LOYALTY

Ali Shakur

© 2018 ANB House of Royalty LLC All rights reserved.

ISBN 978-0-692-13143-5

ANB House of Royalty LLC

2405 Essington Rd STE B106

Joliet,IL 60433

Edited by Dominique Lambright of DML Editing

Printed in the United States of America

Ali Shakur

Prologue

Summer of 2010, and graduation is just around the corner. I'm having one hell of a successful school year at Lake Shore Academy. I led the Lake Shore Varsity Basketball team to an IHSA State Basketball Championship, the first one in over 13 years. For me, basketball is life; I got big dreams and big plans for making it to the NBA. At a young age of 17, tall, skinny, 6'3, with a clean-cut fade, they've labeled me the best high school basketball player in the state of Illinois. Sports Center did a dedicated 90-second piece on me called, "Ezekiel Miller-The Future of Basketball."

Even with all the hype around my basketball IQ, I know I can't be successful off basketball alone, I need a plan B, so I make sure to keep my head in the books. Since the start of my freshman year, I've been making high honors and was given a full academic scholarship to attend Howard University. With the support of the

1

whole community behind me, it definitely keeps me motivated. In couple months, I'll be packing my bags and leaving for Washington, D.C. to start a new chapter in my life.

I live in a city named Lake Shore. It's not the greatest place to grow up in, but it isn't the worst. There are a few dangerous pockets here and there; but overall, it's a decent city. It's not overrun with drugs, gangs, or a bunch of other crimes. Still, those elements are very much a part of the city. A few of the local neighborhood kids I know choose to take the gangbanging and the dope selling route. For me, I prefer to keep busy by working on my game over at The Marcus Garvey Gym, and when I'm not over there, I'm most likely at home studying. I refuse to be that stereotypical black teenager from the hood, going to jail or found dead somewhere from making bad choices.

Even with having high honors, I'm not part of the geek squad or anything like

2

that. I'm the top high school basketball player in the state, ranking top 10 in the nation, so yeah, I got some juice. I get asked a lot why I choose to go to Howard University instead of Duke, Michigan State, or a school that was known for their winning basketball program. Attending an HBCU is something I want to experience as a young black man. Their Business School is one of the best, plus I want to be the first person to get drafted by an NBA team that comes from Howard University.

Everybody wants to be considered my friend of some sort; so, when I make it to the top, they can try and claim some part of it. But through all the fake friends, hugs and well wishes, I have that one friend that is consider my brother, Gabriel Richards. G lives with his Grandmother Belle, about five houses down from me. We have been through it all, we been friends as far back as I can remember. His Mom and my Mom were close friends too, so it's only natural that the bond between the two of us is unbreakable.

We're pretty much the same age, and
he's not much shorter than me, maybe 6'1 in
height. I joke about him being mixed with
white or something because of his light skin
tone. If someone asked me to describe G
personality, I'd say he's a fearless
asshole. Never at a loss for words. Whatever
comes out of his mouth when he opens it,
just rolls out. He speaks his mind, even if
it's stupid as hell. I love this dude; I
wouldn't trade him for the world.

Ali Shakur

The Introduction

"I knew who you were, before you knew who you were"

Tuesday after school, walking through our hood just bullshitting around with G, a voice yell out, "Aye yo! What's up lil niggas! Bring yawl asses over here!"

Squinting my eyes, unable to tell who's yelling from a distance. G takes off jogging across the street, glancing back towards me, waving me on, "Come on nigga, that's JD! Let's go see what he wants."

JD is a real live dope boy. He got a fly ass chick, a dope ass Mercedes Benz, and he rocks nothing but the finest gold jewelry that money could buy. At the age of 25, JD is considered an OG in the hood; he's continually showing love to everybody, young or old. He's really a good dude; his heart is in the right place. Not too many people can say anything negative about him. He took a particular liking to me and G, he tries to do whatever he can to keep us out of trouble. From time to time he'll sit us down and hit us with some type of knowledge or advice, if not both. You can say he's like a big cousin to us.

We approach his Benz, and he hands G a black book-bag. "Do me a favor. I need yawl to go up North and drop this off for me."

G, rubbing his hands together, "Yo, my nigga, you know I fuck with you, right? But going up North ain't no quick trip. Let me drive the Benzie up there and you got deal!"

JD's laughing as he taps my arm, "What's wrong with yo boy, Zeke?"

Shrugging my shoulders, "Shit, I been telling everybody the nigga crazy, but hey, nobody listens to Zeke."

G flips his middle finger, "Yoah okay! Fuck yawl!"

Slightly grinning, JD says, "Aye, seriously, I need yawl to do this for me, and I'll hook yawl up with something. But on some real shit, ain't no bullshitting around with this. Get it there as soon as possible!" It's not unusual for JD to ask us to go do shit for him. Most of the time he just wanted us to go to the store and grab him some snacks or go over to Harold's to get him some chicken wings, and he would give us a few dollars whenever we did.

G starts to unzip the bag, "What's in this bitch?"

JD demeanor changes from being cool and chill to being serious as he snatches the bag away from G. "Aye, I can't be having yo lil ass acting like a fucking kid. Don't either one of you lil niggas open this. All you need to do is get to this address on the paper and drop it off." He points at G, "No stopping to fuck around with them young ass hoes. Just do what I ask. Please. Can you handle that?"

G takes the book-bag, puts it on his shoulders, "Yeah, yeah, we got this negro!" The lifestyle JD lives is not the lifestyle for me. I can't envision myself as a drug dealer, or anything else that brings about negativity to our people. JD is cool and all, but shit, somethings you just gotta say no to. Granted he just wants us to drop something off, but why doesn't he take it himself? My gut is telling me the book-bag that G is holding has either a large quantity of drugs or a lot of money, if not both.

Pulling G closer to me, to speak with him privately. "You sure you trying to do this? Why this nigga can't go do it himself?"

"Come on Zeke, you gotta be fucking kidding me! Stop being paranoid, all we got to do is drop it off. You acting like he's asking to sell a kilo of dope or something. I'm doing the shit, with or without you." He smacks the back of my neck, "Come on pop tart, put on yo big boy pantics." G, never the one to miss an opportunity to get money or to get some pussy, and since I can't see myself convincing him otherwise, fuck it! I'm riding with him right or wrong.

JD approaches, "So yawl finish having yawl debate? Time is of the essence. So, What's the deal? You got me on this or not? Tell me something." G wraps his arm around

JDs shoulder, "Yeah, we got you! But first let's talk about compensation and travel arrangements!" JD laughs, "You'll get paid once the drop is completed. And you're not driving my dam car! You better take yo ass up the street and get them bikes."

North Lake Shore is about an hour and 30-minute bike ride from where we live. I'm not tripping on distance, shit me and G done travel all through Lake Shore on our bikes, but North Lake is where all the rich folks live. Who the hell does JD know that lives up that way?

We follow the directions and end up riding down an alley, stopping at the back of a large brick building. I look towards G with uncertainty, "Is this the place?"

G drops his bike on the ground, holding the bag by its straps without looking away from the building, "Come on Zeke, let's do this shit." I knock on the door, after a few minutes, this big black bald guy opens the door. This motherfucker is at least 6'9, weighing about 270 plus pounds. He's standing inside the doorway, staring, with a mean look on his face. He asks what the fuck we want. This motherfucker's voice sounds like rolling thunder; it's thick, raspy, and fucking intimidating. I ask him if he is Hugo, with the nervousness in my voice apparent.

"Who the fuck wants to know?" He asks stepping out of the doorway. I begin to stutter trying to get the words to come out. G steps up full of confidence. "Chill out with all that aggression fam, we're only here because we got this book-bag for some nigga named Hugo. JD told us to bring it to him, we don't want any problems or misunderstandings, so either you're Hugo, or you're not, and if you're not, then go get him."

He steps up in G's face, "Who the fuck is you supposed to be lil nigga?" G takes a couple steps back, waving his hand in front of his nose.

"First off, don't get in nobody's face with that breath smelling like shit. It's unsanitary my nigga. Breath smelling shitty baby diapers. Secondly, like I said before, I'm here to give this bag to Hugo and not some black ass bald headed Isaac Hayes looking dude." G begins laughing, "Aye Zeke? This nigga looks like burnt microwave bacon!" The big guy gives a grin, coughs up some mucus, and spits on the ground just barely missing G's foot. He steps back into the doorway slamming the door shut.

I push G moving him off balance, "Dude you're a fucking idiot."

G starts laughing out loud, "Why? You think he was going to lay hands on us? Nah Zeke, he ain't going to hurt no kids. Calm down College Boy, we good." G has this nonchalant way of talking which sometimes irritates the shit out of me. He walks over to sit down on the stairs as I sit on my bike waiting for the next move.

"G, do you ever just stop and think before you speak? You know that motherfucker would have whooped your ass, right?"

G, looking down at his phone, "Come on pop tart, the day I get my ass whip will be the day Jesus makes his return, it just ain't happening my nigga."

A few minutes go by, and we're still waiting outside this building; throwing rocks at the abandoned building that's across the alley and arguing about who looks better, Meagan Good or Lauren London. This shit is ridiculous; picking up my bike, I tell G, "Fuck it! Let's Go. Ain't nobody coming out." G passes me the book-bag. As he's about to jump on his bike, the big guy opens the door and tells us to come in.

We're following this dude down a barely lit hallway. Where the fuck is he taking us? I'm a little uneasy about being here. I'm almost certain JD would never put us in a fucked-up situation. Everything's probably cool, and I'm just being paranoid, but then again, I don't know. We've come up to a tall black door, before we enter, the big guy turns to us and says, "Don't touch shit!" He opens the door, and we walk into a big ass

room! The carpet is the color of a dark
blood red, there are gold statues of lions,
and old ancient artifacts, probably worth
thousands of dollars. The ceiling and walls
are designed with angels with devil horns
and demons with halos. We approach this long
wood-grain desk with a wall full of security
monitors right behind it.

There appears to be a man sitting in a
leather chair similar to a king's throne,
with gold and silver trimmings, watching the
monitors. Standing in front of this table,
unable to get a good look at the man sitting
in the chair because the broad back of it is
blocking our view. Heavy smoke is slowly
rising up from the chair, as we stand
clueless.

The big guy walks over to the man in
the chair and whispers something. They
briefly exchange some words as the man turns
his chair to face us. A muscular built,
maybe 5'11 bald Puerto Rican guy dressed in
navy blue slacks, with a neatly tucked white
button-down shirt, stands up. He doesn't

speak; he's puffing on his cigar, staring at us both. I'm trying to look calm, but I'm on the verge of shitting bricks. Glancing over at G, I notice the motherfucker is grinning, as if our lives may not be in danger. Motioning my head for him to say something. G busts out laughing, asking the man if he's Hugo. Taking another puff of his cigar, he speaks with a strong Latin accent, "Yes, yes my friend, yes I am Hugo Del La Cruz, and I understand you have something for me. But may I ask, what do you find so amusing?"

G hands the bag over to Hugo, "No disrespect but you're sitting in this motherfucker acting like your Tony Montana or somebody! Who the fuck is you supposed to be, Scarface? I feel like I'm in a fucking movie right now! This joint is crazy!"

Putting my head down, shaking it in disbelief. Hugo grins at the big guy and says something in Spanish. Hugo, with a smirk, gazes over at me, "Your friend has big cojones. How about you? You no speak?

You no big cojones?" I'm trying to avoid making eye contact with him.

"Yeah, I speak. I'm just not sure what to think about… Well, this situation is not something I normally find myself in, and to be honest, I'm a little scared."

As he opens the bag, he says, "There is no need to fear, I am a friend." Looking inside the bag, with a grin, Hugo looks up, nods his head in approval at us both. He hands the big guy the bag and says, "Bear, get our new friends a beverage."

Quickly interrupting, "Nah we're good, we got to go. We have school in the morning, and it's already getting late." Hugo waves Bear off, motions to the two chairs in front of the desk and tells us to sit. He relights his cigar and continues to stare. G leans forward in his chair, and begins to introduce himself to Hugo, but is instantly interrupted. "I know who you are Gabriel Richards and I most certainly know Mr. Ezekiel. The Michael Jordan of high school basketball. Full scholarship to Howard

University." Me and G look at each other in shock. This shit is crazy! I ask how he knows us? He responds, "I am like the all-seeing eye. I knew who you were, before you knew who you were and you're here only because I sent for you."

G sits back, crosses his arms, "Why you sending for us? We don't know you." Hugo adjusts his chair to sit down.

He stares at G and without flinching G stares back. "Gabriel, God's most favorite angel. The messenger of God."

"G, I prefer to be called G."

Hugo grins. "Ahh, of course, G." Hugo shifts his attention towards me. "You're leaving for college soon; you'll be off living on your own. Trying to make your own way in life, but my friend, America is a dog eat dog world and if you want to be able to survive, mi amigo, you got to be ruthless in your approach. I want you to survive my friend, I want you to live the American Dream, but to do so, you need to have money. The type of money that will give you everything you desire in life. Money that will give you power, and from that power you will get absolute freedom. My friend, you have a real opportunity to grab the world by its neck and live out your truest desires." He places his cigar in the ashtray. "No need to wait for a big NBA contract."

G glances over to see if I'm going to say something, he clears his throat, "So, let me get this straight, you're out here just, out granting niggas three wishes and shit?"

Hugo laughs, "You are absolutely right my friend. I want to offer you the keys that will unlock any door you wish to open." Hugo opens a drawer on the desk and takes out a set of three golden keys. "Each key represents the three things every man desires. Power, money and respect! Come, be a part of my family. Live life with no limits."

Completely caught off guard with his request. "Look, Hugo, I can't get involved in this shit. No disrespect, but I got too much to lose."

Hugo smiles, his teeth bright white, outlined in gold. "You're afraid of losing your school? My dear Ezekiel, your school, will not go anywhere. I'm simply just, enhancing your way of living. You have more to gain then you have to lose."

G looks at Hugo; then he looks at me, looks back at Hugo, "So wait?!? All this shit you're talking about, is it for real or you just bullshitting?" Hugo gets up, grabs the three golden keys and tells us to walk with him.

As we're walking through the hallway, Hugo tells us that we're family and will be treated as such. He claims he will give us the freedom to do whatever we wanted in life. Absolute freedom! How is that even possible? This shit got me bugging the fuck out right now! What in the hell did JD get us into?! Who the hell is Hugo supposed to be!? Why the fuck would he send us straight into the lion's den? G walks along side of

Hugo, as I walk behind them looking around trying to remember every small detail, in case I need to plan our escape. Hugo stops at another door. "Ezekiel, I want you to open the door." I turned the doorknob, but the door doesn't open. It's locked. Hugo pulls out one of the golden key and hands it to me. "That key you hold in your hand, is the key to the unlock the door to absolute freedom."

I put the key in, unlocked the door, and my eyes get wide, as my mouth drops to the floor! The black light in the room illuminates the plush carpet that designs the floor, the walls, and the ceiling. A room of beautiful women of all flavors. Black women, Latin women, Asian persuasion, big ass white girls! Ass and titties are bouncing everywhere! I look over to where I think G is standing, but he's already made his way to a couch, surrounded by women shaking their asses and kissing on him. As I looking across the room, I start feeling a level of excitement. A Latin woman with her big titties hanging out walks up, grabs me by the hand and leads me to another couch, where she began kissing me all over. I hear Hugo say have your fun, as he closed the door. G yells over, "Aye Zeke, I know you can get used to this, my nigga!" The music is playing, the women are dancing, and the sexual vibe increases. Shit, it's a fucking buffet in here, anything I want, I get. It's like I'm a King! I must admit, I'm loving this shit, and I know damn well G is too. Every sexual desire a man could imagine is being fulfilled. There are no limits to what these women are willing to do.

We're in this room for what seems like forever. Hugo walks in, claps his hands, the women get up and walk out, leaving us with our pants at our ankles. Quickly pulling our pants up as Hugo walks towards us, he hands us both envelopes that contain seven hundred and fifty dollars, he says to us, "Absolute freedom. Now it's time for you to go." G gets all excited once Hugo hands us the envelopes. Two of his favorite things in life, money and bitches. G takes the money out the envelope and stuffs it in his pocket. Without even knowing why Hugo was offering us so much or without even asking what we had to do, G says to Hugo he's down, and I'm not sure why, I know I shouldn't, but I agree with G.

G asks when we can start. Hugo looks at us both, takes a couple puffs of his cigar and says, "You started the moment you walked through my door. Now follow me, I must get you home. You have school in the morning."

We enter Hugo's garage, which is full of all types of cars, trucks, motorcycles, and a couple speedboats. Hugo places his hands behind his back as he stands in the doorway. He instructs for Bear to take us home. "Wait! What about our bikes?" I ask.

Bear unlocks the doors to the truck, "Get them tomorrow."

We end up getting dropped off at my crib about 9:00 pm. Sitting in my room recapping today's events. G is amped up sitting in the chair twirling my basketball in his hands, "Yeah nigga I'm about to get paid, I'll have all the bitches on my dick. I'm about to go buy me a Maybach first thing in the morning and throw some 26's on that bitch, have her looking real classy!"

Walking over to my bedroom door and closing it. "First off G, you have school in the morning. Secondly, you failed Driver's ED three times my nigga; you have no license! You can't drive, and you can't buy a fucking Maybach for seven hundred dollars my nigga. You're tripping! Plus, you don't even know what the nigga want us to do."

"Fuck you Zeke! You always crushing a nigga hopes and dreams and shit. A motherfucking dream crusher, that's all you are! Why you always hating?"

"I'm not hating, but let's not lose sight of what we planned. The nigga sells dope and but the looks of shit, he ain't selling a little bit either. This not who we are. I don't even know why I agreed to that dumb shit. But either way, we're in and out in. We get this money, stack it and get the fuck outta here!"

G shoots the ball in the dirty clothes basket, "Yes sir, blah blah blah. Aye Zeke, seriously though, I saw you eating that bitch booty! You can't ask me for no more hits on my drinks. Nigga your new name is CBT!"

"CBT? What the fuck does that mean?"

G bust out laughing, "Captain Booty Tongue! You out here licking bitch's booties."

We both laugh. "Hold on G, I know you ain't trying to crack jokes, because you know I got jokes too nigga."

"Yeah, yeah, I know nigga you got jokes, and you also got shit crumbs on your motherfucking lips."

He's laughing hysterically at his own jokes and the shit ain't even that funny. "G! Get out of my room, go home. Right now!"

"Aww, you sitting over there mad with yo, I eat booty face?! I'm tired of being here anyway. I'll see you tomorrow Pop Tart!"

The end of the school day bell rings, and we're walking out of school. The black Cadillac from last night is waiting for us in the student parking lot. Without second guessing we get in, and Bear drives off. We're in the back seat heading towards Hugo's office. Jokingly G say's to Bear, "Has anybody ever told you that you're an ugly motherfucker? You probably don't get no pussy! Not even from the bitches Hugo has walking around asshole naked."

Bear looks up through the rearview mirror, "Ask your Mom about me."

G lunges at Bear, but I pull him back down before he could do anything. Bear smiling, his reflection in the rearview, not flinching for a second continues driving. G is pissed off by the disrespect from Bear. "Nigga, watch your mouth disrespecting my Mama. She's dead, them the games I don't play. Fuck around and get a mouth shot!" G's Mom passed away about 4 years ago, in a car accident. The police said a drunk driver fell asleep at the wheel and hit her car head-on, she died on impact. G's father has never been around. From what I understand G's mama knew who he was, but G never met him, and she didn't want him to either. G mentioned that he received a letter from his pops shortly after his Mom passing. The letter said he was coming out to Lake Shore to finally meet G, but his dad never showed up, and G never heard from him again. He blames himself for his Mom's car accident since it happened while she was on her way to watch one of our basketball games.

G played his freshman year at Lake Shore, but after the accident, he couldn't bring himself to play again. G, nor Grandma Belle, found out about his mother passing until the next day when they woke up to the police knocking at their door. Up to that point, G thought his Mom missed his game because she was working late hours at the hospital. A tragic situation that left a part of him empty.

We pull into the garage and follow Bear to Hugo's office. He's acting as though he's happy to see us, sitting down in the same chairs from the night before. Hugo begins to explain what he expects of us. The number one rule that trumps all other rules is that he demands loyalty.

He instructs us to never attract any attention to ourselves, attend school like we've been doing, and do whatever it is that we do on a typical day to day basis, nothing needs to change. When he needs us, he will instruct Bear to send us a text with the address for the pickup. Once we pick up the book-bag, we're to come here and hand it to Hugo. Exactly what JD had us do yesterday. Hugo says he will only need us maybe three or four days a week, directly after school.

Hugo's very convincing in his approach. "To the naked eye, you're just two kids riding through town on your bikes with backpacks. You'll fly under the radar, dinero fácil mi amigo. My friends, this is an opportunity of a lifetime. If you do well, I will reward you with things you can only dream of. All I ask for in return is your loyalty to me and my family." Hugo extends his hand for us to shake it. If this is all we had to do, how bad could it be? I mean, what he wants us to do doesn't sound bad. Nobody would expect us to be out picking up and dropping drugs or money. I can handle this. What's the worst that can happen? Shit, I can use the extra cash for school anyway. Slowly, I reach my hand out and shook Hugo's hand in agreement.

Weeks went by, and we quickly built up the trust of Hugo while getting paid in the process. Working for Hugo is decent, he's treat us like kings, he doesn't get annoyed or frustrated with G's smart-ass mouth like most adults would. We're living the good life, just as Hugo had promised. The connections that Hugo has allows us to go almost anywhere in Lake Shore, or any other surrounding cities and not have to pay for anything.

Free food at some of the most beautiful exclusive restaurants around town, free courtside tickets to the Chicago Bulls game, backstage passes to concerts, and unlimited access to the Plush Room. Hell, whenever we want to go out to kick it, he'll throw us the keys to the Ferrari 458 Italia. We don't worry about anybody fucking with us, because Hugo kept his bodyguards close by. It's feels like Lake Shore is just one big playground. A playground that belongs to us. If this is what it feels like to be a superstar, then I can't wait to make it to the NBA.

I did an excellent job of hiding everything I was into away from my Mom. I don't want her to start asking questions about my whereabouts, or the coming home late. My Mom isn't overprotective, she allows me to do what I want because she knows I wouldn't be out causing trouble.

So, giving her money to help with bills, the clothes, and the shoes didn't raise any concerns with her; it's not like

28

I'm out here buying anything or doing stuff that's outside of my character.

Overall, Hugo turns out to be cool, he jokes around with us, and as a gift, he puts in an authentic full-size NBA basketball court in the lower level portion of his office building. Everything is going great right now, but no matter how great things are at the moment, I'm still planning on going to college in the fall. In the meantime, I'm enjoying the summer, the women, the money, and the freedom to do whatever I want, without any repercussions.

In Too Deep

"When you think of something or someone so powerful, that can bring both Jesus and the Devil to their knees, who is it that you first think of?"

Saturday morning, me and G are out at the park shooting hoops when Bear pulls up in a Phantom Rolls Royce. He opens the back-passenger door, Hugo steps out wearing a tailor fitted two-piece dark red suit, with his shades on, puffing on a cigar. Hugo doesn't dress like the typical drug dealer that I've ever seen. He has this very professional business look about himself. A different look than how JD dresses. Hugo tells G to come get in the car and take a ride with him. G bounce passes me the ball. I can tell he's a little shocked by the request. He starts grabbing his things, but mention for me to meet him at Pete's Corner Store. Grabbing him by his arm I ask, "You sure you want to get in the car with this dude alone?"

"Zeke, chill out. If I'm not at Pete's in 30 minutes and you don't hear from me. Then that's when you start worrying." G grabs his Gatorade and heads toward Hugo. I run towards the hoop, lay the ball up, and jog to where they're standing. Breathing slightly heavy, I ask Hugo, "What's up? Is everything cool?"

"Yes, everything is great my friend. I need to speak with Gabriel. Alone. You'll have your moment when the time comes. Until then go practice your hoops." I watch as they drive off. He'll be okay, hopefully. Ain't no need to stress over it, so I went back to practicing on my game.

Fifteen minutes' pass, and I grab my gym bag and begin walking to Pete's Corner Store. As I'm walking up the street, I see Liz coming out the nail salon. Liz is JD's girl, and she's a thick ass redbone. I haven't seen JD around since we took the bag over to Hugo. It's only a couple places he would post up at, but he wasn't seen at any of his usual spots. Walking up to Liz, I give her a hug and ask, "What's been up with JD? Why hasn't he been around?" Liz checks the time on her MK watch, looks around, then ask where I was walking to. "Up to the corner store right up the street."

Smiling, she asks, "Do you mind if I walk with you?" As we're walking, she began to tell me that JD was arrested on drug trafficking charges and would probably end up doing 12 years in the federal penitentiary if convicted. Since he made bail, he's been staying off the grid trying to keep a low profile. This is my first time ever hearing of JD being locked up before. He didn't do the hand to hand transactions like the corner guys, or the small-time drug dealers, he's somewhat of a significant player in the game. Looking at Liz it's apparent that she's worried about JD, but it was nothing she could do, but wait and see what would happen.

Liz is a sweetheart, she wasn't some local hoe that got with JD because of the status it would bring. She wants JD to go legit, open a mentor center or a legit business, but when you been selling dope all your life with no real educational background, going legit is a hard dream to make a reality for some. Liz didn't come in the store with me, she continued her way.

Waiting around for G, outside Pete's, the Rolls Royce finally pulls up, and he gets out. I'm curious to know what Hugo wanted, but G's hesitant to talk about it. He grabs the bag of chips out of my hand. "Man, that nigga was talking to me about the importance of loyalty and if I ever need anything to let him know because we're family, and a bunch of other bullshit. Hugo ain't who we think he is Zeke, but… I don't know man. It's a lot of shit on my mind right now." G is holding back something and I can't figure it out, but something was different about him. Or maybe it's just me. Maybe I'm just reading too much into it.

10:00 am the next morning, I step out on the front porch to get some fresh air. At the end of the block, there's a bunch of police cars, ambulances, and a crowd of people. As I walk down there to see what's going on, a flow of sadness begins to creep in as I get closer. Holy shit! JD is slumped over his steering wheel! Dead! The whispers from within the crowd are, somebody walked up and shot him multiple times. The Benz is shot up, he took a bullet to the head, the blood is still oozing from the wound. Blood is splattered all over the front windshield, and the side windows are entirely shot out.

His head is down on the steering wheel with his eyes still wide open. It's like he's staring straight at me. Stunned by what I'm seeing, I stand, staring back at him. Looking around into the crowd of people that had gathered, the sadness and disbelief are all around. Girls hugging one another crying, guys sitting on the curb with their head in the palms of their hands. Wait, there is another body near the front end of

the Benz! The body is covered in a white
sheet, I hear somebody say that's Liz under
the sheet. Damn! I just saw her yesterday,
and now she's dead. The scene is crazy,
everybody has their own speculations about
what happened. The Detectives are walking
through the crowd asking questions, but
nobody's willing to talk. JD and Liz being
people I know personally, makes holding back
my tears and trying to keep my cool a hard
thing to do.

    I call G to tell him to come down here,
but no answer. JD wasn't involved with any
of that gang shit, and I never seen him
really lose his cool, but I'm not with him
twenty-four seven. Everybody talks about
being a real nigga, but JD was a real one,
even though he sent us to Hugo. Knowing how
JD looked out for us daily, and now knowing
Hugo, I don't think he had a choice in the
matter. As a testament to the love that JD
got for us, there was a situation G had with
the Four Corner Hustlers, the local street
gang that thinks they rule the fucking

world. G was fucking with Tray baby mama, it had got to the point where Tray wanted to kill him and me, even though I don't have anything to do with who G is fucking.

Tray and a bunch of his niggas had posted up across the street from where G lives, waiting for one of us to come out. G may have done a lot of stupid shit, but he knew going outside would've gotten him fucked up. We stayed inside G bedroom as he yelled continuous fuck you's out the window. Guns were pointed at us, gang signs were being thrown up, Tray wasn't leaving until he got to one of us. I called JD and told him what was going on, he came right over no questions asked. He pulls into the driveway with another guy in the car, they walked across the street to Tray. I don't know what was said, but Tray and his niggas got in their cars and left. As he walked back towards his car, JD looked up towards the window and yelled, "You lil niggas stay the fuck out of trouble." Both JD and the guy he was with started laughing as they got back in JD's car and left. We never had any issues with Tray afterward. No matter what JD did in his life, he always made sure we were straight. I guess you can say he was more than a big cousin, he was like a big brother to us.

They began cleaning up the crime scene when I start walking back home. Still haven't heard from G, so I sit down on my front porch to send him another message. Then out of nowhere, I hear, "Motherfuckers was on that bullshit!" Looking over I see G walking from the side of my house.

"Nigga! Where the fuck you been?"

G takes a seat in the chair next to mine. He stares out across the street where a couple of kids were playing. He yawns, "I was fucking with Leila. You know ole girl with that fat ass that was up at Shamrocks the night before last? That crazy bitch is a real freak! I had to pop a couple dick pills just to keep up." He starts laughing with his head down. Glancing over at me he says, "I heard some stick-up kids from out East put them bullets in him." Still in shock and filled with sadness, I describe how the scene looked when I was there and how JD looked as he laid slumped over in his car, but G doesn't seem bothered about the death of a friend.

A week had passed since JD's murder. We both attended the funeral, there must've been hundreds of people that showed up to pay their respects. That just goes to show how much love JD had in the hood, but just because you give love to the streets doesn't mean the streets are going to love you back. RIP Big Homie.

Tuesday night, I'm sitting at the desk in my room finishing up some homework. My phone goes off, and it's a text message from Bear. He's on his way to pick me up. It's kind of weird that Hugo wants to see us at night, especially after 8:00 pm. He never wants us to work at night, even when we offer to do pickups. He would decline by saying tomorrow is a new adventure. I gather up my homework, put it all in my book-bag, ran down the stairs and out the front door. Looking up and down the street to see if I can see G coming. Bear pulls up and tells me to get in. Bear is the type of dude that doesn't talk much. He's Hugo chief enforcer, and I guess his second in command. He doesn't have the desire to communicate with me or G. Hell, now that I think about it, I never seen him really communicate with anybody other than Hugo. So, me trying to talk to Bear is like talking to a brick wall. If he does speak, it is either him answering a question with another question or giving three or four-word answers.

I asked Bear if he wants me to call G? He looks at me in the rear-view mirror with a slight grin, "Nah, he chilling." From this point on, I'm a just sit back and stare out the window. The route is opposite of the way to the office, where we usually meet at, so I'm not sure where he's taking me. Are we even in Lake Shore anymore? The scenery changes from being in the city to being on the freeway, to driving through a dark forest; I see absolutely nothing besides trees. The only light is the lights from the truck. Anxious to know where I'm being taken, I ask Bear again where the hell we were going, but he says nothing. He just looks at me in the rear-view mirror and continues driving. We're approaching a large gated entrance. I'm looking around trying to see if there are any other buildings or signs, something to give me a clue to where I'm at, but I'm surrounded by darkness and trees.

There's a guard house at the entrance, two armed men walk up on both sides of the truck looking in. Bear shares a laugh with one of the men. Just before we get through the gate, I see on each side two huge statues. One of the sculptures was depicting Jesus on his knees, and another figure that appears to be the devil, also on his knees. Bear drives down another long-wooded road until we reach a big ass mansion. The yard lights are illuminating the house, making it

stand out in the darkness of the night. A
dozen security personnel with guns are
patrolling the grounds. I notice security
walking near a large swimming pool, there's
security walking along the top balcony of
the house and security walking with German
Shepherds. You would think the President or
someone important lives here. As we get
closer to the front of the house, we drive
around a water fountain the size of
Buckingham Fountain. On top of the fountain,
sits a massive statue of a lion.

Pulling up to the front door of the
mansion, one of the security personnel opens
the truck door for me to get out. Walking
into the house, amazed by how everything
looks so shiny and new. A woman walks past
us wearing nothing besides high heels, her
bra, and thong. She smiles at me as she
blows a kiss, I smile back and start to
follow her, Bear grabs me by my shirt collar
stopping me and points straight ahead. We
begin walking through the house. The floor
is made of golden tile with small diamonds

in the middle. Checking things out around me as I follow Bear, peeping into a room where two women are tongue kissing and doing cocaine off each other titties, another room has women performing oral sex on one another. I know Hugo has an abundance of wealth and power, but I imagine that there was some type of limit to how much he possesses. But apparently, he has unlimited resources of both. Everything a man could want in life, Hugo has complete access to it. Priceless artifacts, expensive cars, helicopter, boats and of course plenty of women and money.

He has pictures with some of the most infamous people in the world, past, and present. A portrait of him and Fidel Castro, a picture of him and Hector Camacho, the famous Puerto Rican boxer, but one image has really caught my attention. A picture of a young Hugo with Frank Lucas and Nicky Barnes. Both Frank and Barnes were well known Harlem drug dealers from the late 60's into the 70's. Barnes was the head of The

Council, and Lucas had a drug empire worth over a million dollars. I'm not sure how old Hugo was at the time, but he must have had a lot of power and influence to get both Frank and Nicky in the same picture. I don't think there is a picture that exists anywhere today with both Nicky and Frank together, besides the one that's on Hugo's wall.

We walk down a corridor that leads us into a dining room. Hugo, with G, sits at the table laughing. Walking in confused and uneasy. I wasn't expecting G to be here. "Yo, what's up G?" He nods his head what's up.

Hugo stands and says, "Come, join us, my friend, we been waiting for you." Taking a seat across from G, he looks at me smiling. Hugo lights up his cigar, "Como esta amigo? In English, how are you, my friend? I know you're wondering why I called you here tonight. I've been in Lake Shore for a quite some time, and the potential to transcend my family business to new heights is unimaginable. I am a man with vision,

43

which means good things, not only for me but for you two as well. Mas dinero y mas ponder. More money, more power. But I have a problem, those pesky street rats and their peddling of drugs. No es bueno, very very bad for my business. They bring down market value."

I sit upright in my chair, "But hold on Hugo. That's like the pot calling the kettle black. Because you're a drug dealer. Am I, right?" G mumbles dumb ass under his breath. Hugo doesn't immediately respond. There's a silence that falls, there's a feeling of uncertainty about my comment.

He stands puffing on his cigar, staring at me as though he sees right through me. "Ezekiel, I'm not what you would call a drug dealer. I don't stand on street corners waiting for crack fiends. I have many businesses, businesses that expand to the far and darkest regions of the world. Businesses that are worth more than millions of dollars. Have you ever heard a drug dealer talk about paying taxes on owned

properties or on businesses that they own?
I'm no drug dealer, my friend. I'm what you
would call a businessman. So, I advise you
not to get the two confused again."

Shifting in my chair nervously. He's
apparently upset with me calling him a drug
dealer. In an attempt to change the awkward
tension at the table. I apologize for
labeling him a drug dealer and then asks
what was up with the two statues at the
front gate. The figures of Jesus and the
Devil on their knees. He looks at G with a
grin, walks over to his liquor cabinet,
pulls out a bottle of tequila, pours some in
a glass, walks over and hands it to me.
"When you think of something or someone so
powerful, that can bring both Jesus and the
Devil to their knees, who is it that you
first think of?"

Taking a sip of tequila, I reply,
"God."

"I like the name Hugo better my
friend." G starts laughing, Bear walks in,
whispers to Hugo, and with a smile, Hugo

pats Bear on the back and tells him to bring the visitor in. Shortly after, a short fat black guy with a taper fade and a full beard walks in. He wears a pair of black tightly creased slacks and a black button-down with a pair of black alligator skin dress shoes, and in his hand, he carries a briefcase. Leaning forward to ask G if he's seen this guy before, he shakes his head no. They shake hands, and Hugo introduces him as Fat Tony from the Bronx. When Fat Tony speaks, you can clearly hear his New York accent.

G looks at Hugo confused, "Really? I thought NY niggas wore Tim's."

Fat Tony looks at Hugo, "Who the fuck is this kid?"

G quickly responds, "Why are you asking him when I made the comment and I'm sitting right here?"

Tony places the briefcase on the table and focuses his 5'6 chubby frame towards G. "Look B. Don't get fucked up in front of your people." G jumps up, but before he could say anything, Hugo tells him to have a seat and show respect.

G, flopping back down in his seat, "To get respect you gotta earn respect, and right now this nigga ain't earning shit."

"True enough Gabriel," Hugo says as he opens the briefcase. "Fat Tony has done enough to earn my respect, and in due time you all will learn to respect each other. Not only does he make sure my business in the whole New York tristate area is being conducted to my liking, but he is also the Superior King of the Black Kings, which is the most ruthless group of young businessmen on the east coast. I brought him here to help with my vision, so I need you and Ezekiel to be courteous to our guest for the time he is here." Hugo doesn't give details about his vision with me and G, but I'm sure it has something to do with his businesses. G sits in his chair still upset as Hugo and Tony talk about their business relations. Pouring me another glass of tequila, I sit back in my chair waiting to go home.

A Fresh Start

"Are you going to grab my hand, or just wait
for it to fall off?"

A few days after being at Hugo's home and meeting Fat Tony, I'm sitting in Mrs. Parker's math class when she tells me that I'm needed in the Dean's office. Walking into Mr. Ross's office, I stop right before entering through his doorway. My mother and two FBI agents are sitting and waiting for me. Standing in the office doorway, I'm not sure if I really want to walk in. I ask, "What's going on?"

Mr. Ross explains that Special Agent Thomas and Sanchez want to ask me some questions. My Mom nervously says, "Zeke, just be truthful, tell them everything you know. You're not in any trouble baby, I promise. Just tell the truth." As a black man growing up in America, it's hard to trust any type of law enforcement personnel, no matter what they say.

Ali Shakur

Agent Sanchez, a Hispanic man, maybe in his mid-thirties asks if I know a Jason Diggs. "No, I never heard of a Jason Diggs."

"Are you sure? I just want to make sure we're clear on who Mr. Diggs is. You're familiar with JD, right?"

"Yeah, I know of a JD. Why?"

Sanchez opens a vanilla folder and shows me a picture of JD. "Jason Diggs and JD are the same people. Government name & street name."

I tell Sanchez that I've seen JD around the neighborhood, but I didn't know him. Agent Thomas, a black man in his late forties, jumps in forcefully. "Look here boy, the answer is a simple yes or no. Do you or don't you know JD?"

Pausing for a second to gather my thoughts. I'm not trying to say anything that would incriminate me. Clearing my throat, "Yeah, I know him." Looking at both Sanchez and Thomas, "Why the hell do you want to know who I know and don't know?" The nervousness has my leg shaking.

49

My Mom places her hand on my leg. "It's ok baby, I'm here with you." I'm not sure if I'm being investigated for his murder or if they're just asking questions to figure out what I know about JD's death, but either way, I don't have any answers for them. They're asking questions like; Why G and I were seen hanging around JD on almost a daily basis? I shift in my chair, "JD made sure we were okay and that we didn't have any issues with the gangs, and sometimes he brought us food."

Agent Thomas slams his fist on the table. "I'm not buying that shit! You knew he was a known drug dealer, right? How many times did you deal drugs for him?"

Becoming increasingly irritated, which causes me to raise my voice, "Look! I don't know what that man did in his personal life! He was a friend that looked out for me. That's it, that's all. Him being killed was a sad day for me. If you think I know what happened to him, or think I had something to do with it, you got your nose in the wrong direction. Point, blank, period." I'm smart enough to know that if they had anything on me, I would be in handcuffs or either sitting in their office being questioned, but it is strange for the Feds to be interviewing me in the middle of the school day. I ask Sanchez why they're so interested in JD. I knew what Liz had told me before, but I want to hear it from their mouths.

Sanchez brakes it down to me, "JD was arrested for drug trafficking, but he flipped and was working with us in favor of a reduced sentence. JD was our federal informant." Sitting back in my chair crossing my arms in disbelief, I would have never guessed that JD was working with the Feds. I sat in Mr. Ross's office with Thomas and Sanchez for probably an hour. They finally finish up their good cop bad cop routine, and I'm able to leave school for the rest of the day.

As me and my Mom are heading home, she begins crying, telling me about how everything is going great and the evilness in this world will bring me down if I let it. With me about to leave for school, I need to watch the company I keep around, or I can end up losing it all. My Mom's not a religious person, she just believes in doing good to others, so that good will come back. Do wrong and wrong will return. My Mom is a 3rd-grade teacher at Scotts Elementary School, and my father passed away when I was about nine years old. He was misdiagnosed and given medication that eventually shut down his vital organs. But before that happened, he was a Sergeant in the Air Force Reserve. The death of my father was hard on my Mom and me. My dad was the rock of the family and my role model. Mom kept us from falling apart after his death, even when she seemed like she was stressed and tired. She's a strong black woman from Mississippi, and she does whatever it takes to keep our heads above the water.

I wonder how G is holding up at school. If the Feds questioned me, I'm positive that they're going to challenge him as well. What would Hugo do or say if he knew about the Feds asking us questions? As soon as I got home, I sent a text to G to call me asap. He calls about fifteen minutes later. He sounds shook, he's talking fast about how the Feds were asking questions about JD and his association with him. I'm trying to get him to be cool and stay calm. We didn't do anything besides just kick it with him. But he just keeps on saying "Nah Zeke I need to get out of town. They know man, trust me they know."

"What do they know G? If they knew about the drugs and the money, we would be locked up. Just stay calm, we'll be ok." For me to say that I'm not worried, would be a lie. "G, the Feds are just trying to see who knows what about JD, and with us having a close association with him, we're first on their list, suspect or not."

With everything that happened earlier today with the Feds, I'm almost positive that a text from Bear was coming soon. Later in the evening G comes over, he's a lot calmer than he was when I first talked to him earlier today. I ask if he heard from Hugo or Bear, he says he hasn't heard from anybody. That's strange, a day that we usually do a run for Hugo is the same day we get questioned by the Feds, and Hugo doesn't instruct Bear to reach out to us. Maybe Hugo didn't need us today. Maybe he's not aware of what happened. But wait, Hugo knows pretty much everything that we do. How would he not know that the Feds were asking us questions about a murder that involves a former business partner of his, that we knew personally? Is it possible that JD was going to give up Hugo for that reduced sentence, or was he targeting someone else? Whatever JD had going on, has the Feds focusing their efforts towards us. I can't blame G for being scared, anytime the Feds come asking questions, it's never a good thing. Especially if one of their informants come up dead.

As time goes on, everything starts returning to normal. When I say normal, it means before Hugo came along. I haven't heard from him or Bear, and it does feel good. I do miss the exotic cars, the women, the money, and that feeling of having the freedom to do whatever I want, but that criminal lifestyle, is not the life I want to live. I'm not even sure what happened to Hugo, maybe the Feds got him, or perhaps he went back to Puerto Rico or somewhere. I'm not complaining though, I can finally get back to my regular life. I saved up a few thousand dollars from working with Hugo, and since graduation is right around the corner, I decided to buy me a Jeep. I just want something decent to get me around the city that won't cause unwanted attention since I don't have the muscle of Hugo any more.

Over time, I'm noticing some parts of Lake Shore are starting to look a little different. Nobody is hanging out on the street corners; the abandoned buildings laced with graffiti are being cleaned up and used as office space. The city is under a complete remodel, and I can't say that it's a bad thing, because the negative vibe was decreasing in noticeable amounts. A small pizza delivery service named The Pizza Joint opened a few blocks away from the house. It feels and looks like a whole new city. The community is long overdue for a change, and it's good that it's happening sooner than later. Whoever or whatever is behind this community clean-up needs to stick around for a while to keep it from getting damaged again.

Finally, the day I been waiting for, I made it to the end of another chapter in my life. Today is the day I graduate! I've been looking forward to this day for a very long time. I wish my dad were here to see his son walk across the stage, but I know he is smiling down proud of the man I'm becoming. Checking myself out in the mirror, I decided to keep my graduation fit simple. A pair of blue Jordan's, some black slim fitted jeans, a blue button down to match the shoes and a black blazer to top it off. I'm looking fly as hell, and nobody can tell me differently.

Ali Shakur

A loud horn blows a couple times outside. Peeping out of the blinds of my bedroom window. A stretch Hummer? What's this about? Stepping outside on the front porch waiting to see who was going to get out. The driver comes around and opens the back-passenger door, G steps out the limo with his arms stretched open. "What up fool, we did it!" Laughing, I begin dancing down the stairs. Happy and excited to be able to graduate and start this next chapter. I know both of our parents are proud, especially Grandma Belle. G's chances of graduating were slim to none. Mama and Grandma Belle rode together, and I rode in the Hummer with G.

The graduating class enters the gymnasium, and the cheers are off the meter. Me and some other students are receiving a special award for maintaining a 4.0 GPA during the entire four years of high school. "Ezekiel Miller!" Finally, my name is called to walk across the stage to grab my diploma, more than half the people in the crowd started cheering, but out of all the cheers and yells, I can only hear my Mom's voice saying, "I'm proud of you son."

After the ceremony, we gather near the school trophy case. There's a few females and homeboys that want to take pictures with me and G. It's cool, this may be the last time I see most of these people anyway. Laughing and mingling with some of the other students and people that were in the crowd, I wait on G to figure out what the plan was for the night. My Mom wants to go out for dinner, but G wants to hit up this graduation party out West. So, we're going to bypass the dinner and head to this party.

Pulling up to the party, there is a shit load of people just kicking it outside. The parking lot is bumping! Rubbing my hands together, "Hell yeah G, I'm about to get it in tonight!" Inside, the party it's even more live. Everybody's having a good time, the drinks are flowing, and the hoes are in full force. Navigating my way through the crowd of people, being stopped every few feet by females trying to get with me. One of them is pressing me to come in the bathroom to fuck her, but I'm not on that shit, bitch probably burning or something. Out of all the beautiful ass women that's here, there is one chick that's absolutely gorgeous! I'm guessing she's about 5'3, she got beautiful long black silky hair, milk chocolate skin, and when she smiles, it does something to me that I can't put into words. I swear I'm staring at an Ebony Goddess.

Stepping to her to introduce myself, she smiles and says, "I know who you are, superstar." She turns and walks away. I can't let her get away that easy. Following her outside, she's leaning on the balcony rail looking out into the starry night. I move beside her, also looking into the night. I ask smiling, gazing into her eyes,

"So, do you normally diss superstars or am I the first one?" She laughs, "I'm not interested in being one of your groupies. You got plenty of them already."

Moving in closer to grab her hand gently. As smoothly as possible I say, "All the groupies in the world wouldn't mean anything if I'm with you."

She snatches her hands away, rolls her eyes, "Oh gosh, is that your go-to line?" She busts out laughing. "How many girls have you told that to?" She turns to sit in the lawn chair.

Turning to face her, my back leaning against the rail, "I don't have lines, I think you're the epitome of all things beautiful, and I was hoping to engage in conversation with you. So, let's try this again." Extending my hand out for her to shake it, "Hi I'm Zeke." She hesitates, bats her eyes before shaking my hand. She introduces herself as Alexis. From there, the conversation is flowing so naturally. We're laughing and having a good time getting familiar with one another, that we didn't notice the party was over and people are checking out.

Ali Shakur

Moving through the crowd trying to find out where G is at. I'm calling and texting his phone, but he's not answering. I'm asking people if they saw him, but nobody has since earlier. This shit is pissing me off, we came together, and I'm expecting us to leave out together. The limo is still here, but no signs of him. Maybe he left with some chick, since it was a lot of freaks trying to get it in tonight. Either way, I'm not going to let this limo go to waste.

Alexis is standing out by a car with a group of her girls. I walk over to ask if she wants to go grab a bite to eat with me. Her mouth curves into a little smile, and with attitude, she says, "No! I'm not going anywhere with you alone! You might be a creep or something."

One of her friends says, "Girl you better jump in the car with him." She looks shy and almost scared. Her light brown eyes glistened under the moonlight.

She's still hesitant, so I extend my
hand for her to grab it and hit her with an
ole Billy Dee line. "Are you going to grab
my hand, or just wait for it to fall off?"
She smiles biting her bottom lip, as she
grabs my hand to follow me to the limo. The
driver opens the door for us to get in.
Fuck! Shorty looks good as hell! I don't
know, but it's something different about
her. Maybe I'll play it cool tonight. It's
going to be hard as hell. Shorty body is
banging!

Stopping at a 24-hour diner on the
Westside. We don't stay long, we get our
meal, eat, and leave. Opening the limo door
for her to get in, "Are you ready to go
home?" Checking the time on her phone, "No,
I can hang out with you a little longer."
"Alright cool." The driver takes us around
downtown Lake Shore. Downtown is always full
of traffic and people no matter the time of
day. But instead of just hitting blocks, I
tell the driver to take us to the Hilltop.
The Hilltop is the highest peak in Lake

Shore and the best place to sit and watch the sunrise. I help her get onto the roof of the Hummer so we can watch the sunrise. Grabbing my phone, I play Diary of a Mad Band an album by Jodeci. The mood is set, I put my jacket around her shoulders, before wrapping my arms around her. The smell of her scent is spellbinding. She lays her head on my biceps and with the softness of her voice she says, "Thank you for being a gentleman."

Just as the sun begins to rise over the horizon, I wake her up to ask if she's ready to go home, or did she want to go somewhere else. She pulls out her phone to see the time, "If you don't mind, could you drop me off at my friend Tiarra house? She lives near 1115th and Lowe." On the way there, we don't speak much, she's sleep cuddled in my arms.

Pulling up in front of her friend's house, we say our goodbyes. Moving in to give her a kiss on her lips, she gently pushes me back with a smile, "Zeke, I had a

wonderful time with you. You're truly a
gentleman, but I don't kiss on the first
date. But it is tempting!" She stands on her
tippy toes to give me a kiss on my cheek.
Watching her walk towards the house. She
stops and turns with a smile, "Stop looking
at my booty!" Laughing, I get in the Hummer
and tell the driver where to take me.

It's 8:30 am as I'm pulling up in front
of G's house. I swear this dude better have
a good excuse for ducking out on me last
night. Walking up to the front porch of his
home, he's sitting outside in his pajamas
and slippers eating a bowl of Lucky Charms.
"What's up, why the fuck you leave out on
me?"

"First off," G says as he pours himself
another bowl of cereal, "Don't talk to me
like you're some tough guy. College Boy!
Secondly, I'm a grown ass man, I didn't
think I had to tell you my every move. I saw
you were all over shorty at the party, so I
dipped off with ole girl that had on that

red dress, shorty throat game is ridiculous."

Sitting down in the chair next to him. "Look G, you been on some other shit ever since the Feds came asking questions about JD. You rarely answer my text messages or my phone calls. You have been my homeboy since forever, and if I did something or if something is going on, you know you can talk to me. Right?"

G sits his bowl of cereal on the ground. "Zeke," G says standing up to stretch, "People grow apart, people choose different paths in life. You will always be my homeboy, and nothing will ever change that. I'm going to always have your back." He looks at me dead in my eyes, shrugs his shoulders and goes back to eating his cereal.

"What the fuck does that even mean?"

"Nothing Zeke, it's nothing." I stand up, fix my clothes, and walk down the stairs towards the gate to leave, turning to ask G if he was still coming to DC with me.

Without looking up from his bowl, he says, "We'll see College Boy." I know something is up, I just don't know what. Maybe he's starting to feel some type of way about me leaving for school, but he always said he was moving out there with me, so I don't understand. Either way, I'm leaving in a couple days to get registration done for school, I don't want to go alone, but it looks like I will be.

I'm exhausted by the time I get home. Let me try and get some sleep. Text messages from Alexis wake me up. She's asking if we can hang out today. She must be really feeling me? Replying to the text, I tell her I'm about to freshen up, and I'll be through. She doesn't want me to know where she stays, so we meet up at the bus stop. Damn! She is looking GOOD! She's wearing tight light blue stonewash jeans that grip her thighs and her booty so perfectly, the white low-cut top shows her belly ring and her feminine six pack. Her breast is nice and perky that gently bounces as she walks towards me. Her ponytail is sticking out the back of a Lakers snapback, as a pair of Gucci sunglasses covers her eyes, and her lips looking shiny and plump from the lip gloss. We embrace with a hug, her scent instantly turns me on, my hormones are going berserk right now. Calm down tiger, calm down.

Heading out East to the movie theater to see the reboot of Nightmare on Elm Street. The plan afterward is to go roller skating and grab some pizza. During this time, I find out that she is initially from the east coast and that she's out here with her brother and his girlfriend visiting Lake Shore for a few months. She doesn't know exactly when they're leaving, but she overheard her brother telling somebody that there is a good chance that they will be relocating here permanently. I'm really digging this girl, she's smart, funny, beautiful, she's fresh, and hasn't been tainted by Lake Shore.

Alexis and I have been spending a lot of time together since the night I met her, and I haven't gone a day without seeing or talking to her. My Mom likes the fact I've met someone that's respectful and polite. Whenever she comes to eat dinner at the house, she helps clean off the table and wash dishes. I never dated for real, I got female friends that cater to my needs whenever I say so, but there's something special about Alexis. Is it love? Maybe. Is it lust? It's possible. All I know is I enjoy being around her. She makes me smile, she makes me laugh, and she keeps me grounded and humble.

Driving home from dropping Alexis off, pulling up to a red light near 71st and Harlow. Wait!? Sliding down in my seat, to my surprise, Bear is walking into Moe's Corner Street Tap with Agent Sanchez. It's been over a month since I heard from Bear and Hugo and seeing Bear with Agent Sanchez is pretty fucked up. What the hell is going on? I'm just going to act like I didn't see

that shit and keep it moving. I hope they
didn't see me, I'm not trying to be
recognized by neither one of them. Shit,
truth be told, I never wanted to work for
Hugo to begin with, but sometimes your left
with no other options. Now, since that shit
is dead, there is no way in hell I'm getting
back in it. With just a little over a month
before I head off to school, I just need to
remain focus and away from any bullshit.

Washington DC

"The world is ours for the taking, so let's take that shit."

The sound of gunshots awakens me from my sleep. The shots I heard, sounded like a high-power automatic, maybe like an AK-47. Sirens zoom pass my house as I'm getting up to go check out what's going on. Walking a couple blocks to where the lights are flashing, there are three bodies under white sheets. Asking one of the bystanders what happened. They say somebody drove through and shot Tray and whoever was with him. Tray didn't live around here, but he was well-known. He was only 20 years old, but his street cred made him somewhat feared.

Standing within the crowd when G walks up, "Man, fuck that nigga. He thought he was untouchable, niggas need to know shit is changing and you either on board or you not." I have no idea what this fool is talking about, he just be ranting about shit sometimes that I stop trying to understand him. All the grimy ass bullshit Tray did

throughout Lake Shore, ain't no telling who
smoked his ass, it was only a matter of time
before he got hit. We stay around the scene
until they start putting the bodies in the
coroner vans. G rubbing on his stomach,
"Man, let's go get some food. You trying to
go to Denny's?"

"Yeah. What time is it?"

"It's time to go get something to eat.
Come on, let's go get that piece of shit
truck you got and go get some food."

Sitting in the booth at Denny's,
laughing and talking shit to each other.
"Aye Zeke, so check this out, I been
thinking. I know I been kind of distant or
whatever you want to call it. I just got
other shit going on, and sometimes I'm
focused on other things, but you're my
homeboy, and I'm going to DC with you."

Laughing out, and reaching over the
table to give him dap, "My nigga!"

"Now look Zeke, when we get there, I'm
shooting my shot at all them fine ass

college hoes. So, don't be cockblocking me and shit."

Laughingly I respond, "Cockblocking? Nigga, please. If anything, my name alone will be the reason you get any play. But speaking of females, I met a nice lil dime piece." I haven't told him about Alexis yet, but since we're on the topic of females, here is the perfect opportunity to tell him about her. He becomes a little surprise when I mention her name but says he doesn't have a problem with meeting her. I shoot her a text so she could come to Denny's to sit and chill with us for a minute. She walks in about twenty minutes later, looking as beautiful as ever. I stand to greet her with a smile and a kiss. She slides into the booth to sit near the window when she looks up to see G sitting there, her facial expression changes. She looks uneasy like she's worried about something.

"Is everything okay?" She quickly shifts her attention back to me. "Yes babe, everything's alright. You didn't tell me you were here with a friend. I was kind of caught off guard." Her voice is soft, and her east coast accent sounds smooth and sexy. Clearing my throat and with a smile, "G this is Alexis my woman and Alexis this is my best friend G."

G looks at Alexis with resentment, she gives him a half smile as her eyes drop to the table, refraining from making any eye contact with him. Something is wrong, I start wondering if G sleep with her at one point? But how is that possible? She told me she only been in Lakeshore for a short time before meeting me. G sits in silence looking at his phone for a few minutes before abruptly putting his sunglasses on and throwing his money on the table. Not clear where this whole change of mood is coming from. "G what's up?"

"Nothing, I'll get with you in a minute Zeke." He gives me dap, walks out pushing the door open forcefully. Damn! The shit was rude as fuck, but that is what I've come to expect from him. Alexis is saying something to me, but I'm in my own world. That whole exchange between G and her just gave me this funny feeling in my stomach.

"Zeke I'm sorry, I didn't mean to upset your friend. Zeke? Are you ok?" Lifting my head and staring at her in her eyes, asking her straight up if she ever met G before today. "No Zeke, I would tell you if I did."

Sitting, looking out the window, wondering what if. She puts her hand on my chin, turning my head towards her, "Zeke trust me. Please." Slightly grinning at her as she leans over to kiss me. G knows a lot of women, mostly in some type of sexual manner so I wouldn't be surprised if G came across her at some point. Either way, I'm not going to bash her about it, I trust her and if anything happened before we got together, could I fault her for it? I just hope she's keeping it real with me.

Checking out of Denny's, I'm not sure what we're about to do, but I do need to go get some stuff for the DC trip in the morning. As we're pulling out of Denny's

parking lot, a text comes through on my
phone from G telling me to come pick him up
so we can go to the mall.
Alexis tells me to drop her off at the bus
stop and to text her whenever I'm finished
with G. One thing I can't seem to figure out
is, after all this time of us being
together, she refuses to allow me to pick
her up or drop her off at home.

Walking through the mall with G, he
starts talking about Alexis. "Alexis looks
good fam, but you need to be careful with
her."

"Why? Did you smash or something?
Straight up G, that whole ya dig that
happened at Denny's got me feeling some type
of way."

He stops, shakes his head as he pulls
out his phone. Showing me pictures of naked
females. "Come on Zeke. If I smashed, that
bitch would definitely be in my phone, she a
bad bitch, straight up. You know I would've
told you at the table if I fucked. It ain't
even like that. All I'm saying, she may be

trying to use you to get whatever she trying to get. I know females, you know I know females, and I can tell you she ain't what she appears to be. Just be careful my nigga, that's all I'm saying." Playfully slapping the back of my head, "Come on College Boy, let's go to this jewelry store."

G typically gives good advice when it comes to females, I understand him wanting to look out for me, but I think what I'm building with Alexis is something special. Putting my bags down to check out some of these gold chains, I wave G over to come where I stand. "Aye G, come look at this," pointing down at this gold Cuban link chain. "G this motherfucker is on point! 24 Karat solid gold! I'm about to put this bitch on layaway."

G doesn't seem impressed or excited as me. "Yeah that looks decent, you ain't got thirty-three hundred to pay for it?" I shake my head no. He calls the jewelry clerk over so he can get it out the case.

Ali Shakur

The clerk, a short fat white guy in a suit that's too big, comes over. "Yes, how can I help you, gentlemen?" Rubbing my hands together I point at the Cuban link and asks if I could check it out. "Ahh yes, this beautiful piece has a price tag of three thousand and three hundred dollars. It's one of the finest pieces available, but unfortunately, we don't accept layaway."

He pulls out the link but is skeptical of allowing me to hold it. "Uhh, can I hold it? Can I look at it?"

G chimes in loudly, "Damn nigga! Ain't nobody trying to steal yo shit! What you think, we can't afford your lil shitty ass jewelry?" G's tone is causing the other customers to look in our direction.

The clerk nervously replies, "I didn't say you were, but can you please keep your voice down? You're disrupting other transactions."

"Fuck you and your clown ass store! Zeke, you sure you want this piece of shit chain?"

"If I had the money hell yeah! This motherfucker is dope." G digs into his pocket and slams a rubber band full of money on the counter like he was playing dominoes.

"I bet you thought we were some young, broke ass niggas huh? Nah white boy, we get money over here. Now go ring that shit up and bring me my fucking change you pig nose bastard." The clerk quickly goes to ring up the sale. "Put that shit on my nigga, let me see how it look on you."

Putting the chain around my neck, "Damn this bitch is heavy as hell!" Checking it out in the small mirror on the counter, the clerk walks back over with the receipt and the change.

"Sir you have…"

G sticks his middle finger up and bust out laughing, "Fuck you and your raggedy ass store!"

On the way back to the crib I ask G where did he get that type of money, but in his nonchalant tone, staring down at his phone, "Damn nigga, a thank you would be the more appropriate thing to say. I don't know who's worse, you or Grandma. I buy you niggas things and instead of a thank you I get questioned. Yawl some ungrateful ass coons."

Laughing as I rub on his shoulder, "Thank you, sweetheart, you made big daddy happy!"

Jerking his shoulder away, "Nigga get the fuck off me!"

Our flight is set to leave at eight in the morning, and my plan is to kick it with Alexis for the rest of the night. We end up at my crib listening to music as she's helping me pack my bags. Quickly finishing, we lay back, cuddle and watch the movie Juice. As she lays on my chest, she reaches for her phone to read a text message she just receives. She jumps up in a panic, "I'm sorry Zeke, but I got to go!" She's moving in such a hurry grabbing up her belongings that I couldn't get any answers to my questions. Walking her downstairs to the front door, she gives me a kiss. Her eyes water up, the sadness in her face is undeniable. She apologizes and asks me if I will call her once my flight lands.

"I'm confused Alexis, why are you leaving in such a hurry?"

Gently caressing the side of my face. "Zeke... I... I'm sorry." She closes the door behind her, leaving me to stand, staring at the door wanting to cry. I'm not even sure that I'll ever see her again.

Unable to sleep later that night, tossing and turning, laying here thinking about Alexis. She's the first girl I ever really cared about, the first girl I ever wanted to build with. Maybe G was right, perhaps she's not into me, she just broke my heart, and she doesn't even know it, or maybe she doesn't care.

6:00 am, it's time to leave for the airport and G decides not to answer his phone or any of my text messages. I'm pissed, texting him, calling him back to back and still nothing. If I wait any longer, I run the risk of missing my flight.

Fuck it, let me go ahead and request an Uber because this nigga is on straight bullshit. Just when the Uber pulls into the driveway, a limo pulls up in front of the house. Standing out on the sidewalk with my suitcase, waiting to see who gets out the limo. I have an idea who it is, but still, I wait. A tall black guy gets out, nods his head at me, and opens the back-passenger door.

G steps out wearing a blue tailored fitted suit with some shades on and a drink in his hand. He gets out the car like he's somebody famous, standing there looking around, making a point to show off his diamond gold watch. He takes a sip of whatever is in his cup. "You were about to take a dirty ass Uber to the airport?"

"Nigga fuck you, you didn't answer your phone. I wasn't about to miss my flight because of you."

G leans back on the limo with his legs crossed, "Are you going to stand there bitching or are you going to get your lil sweet ass in the limo, so we can get this over with?"

Grabbing my suitcase, handing it to the Limo Driver and telling the Uber guy I'm straight as I hop into the limo. "What's up with the suit G? You look like a certain somebody."

He gives a little smirk, "I wanted to show your future college peers, that Mr. College Boy superstar, has a world-renowned genius marketing slash sports agent, but every time I attempt to show you that I got your back, you always question me. What do you want me to do Zeke?" There's tension brewing between us, but I'm not trying to let this trip end up being fucked up.

"Look G, I apologize for not appreciating everything you do. I got a lot going on right now, and I'm at a stage in my life that I just want things to flow perfectly."

"Yeah well don't come at me like I'm the bad guy." G throws back whatever was left in his cup and howls like a wolf. "Now let's get this shit cracking my nigga!"

Turning up the music and bouncing to the beat, "My nigga, pour me a shot of that Hennessy, shit is about to get real!" And just like that, we were back on the same page.

They call our names over the loudspeaker in the airport telling us to come to the front desk. G leans over and says loud enough for other people to hear, "They finally figured out you're a fucking terrorist."

Pushing him away from me, "Come on G, you think you could of have said that any louder? You know these white people be tripping when it comes to that shit." We move through the crowded area and approach the customer service desk. "Hello, I'm Ezekiel Miller," I say politely.

The lady behind the counter asks G if his name is Gabriel Richards. "The one and only baby, what's up?" G says as he moves his lips in a kissing motion towards her.

We show her our identification, she says, "Please follow me, gentlemen." She takes us to the Flight Attendant that's standing at the entrance. "Please follow her and she'll escort you to your seats."

I look at G, "What the hell is going on?"

"Why you asking me? I'm following you." He pats me on my back, "Let's go pop tart." Following the Flight Attendant as she escorts us to first class seating. She tells us whatever we want, just push the button, and someone would be over immediately to address our needs. As people began to board the plane, some of them turned their nose up at us. There's a white couple seated across from us that keeps glancing over like we aren't good enough to be here. What really pissed them off is when the Captain came over to us and shook our hands. He says to us, "Enjoy the flight gentlemen as we will be taking off shortly." He walks into the cockpit without speaking to the other first-class people. G looks over at the white couple, the woman asks if we're rappers or entertainers. I start laughing. G says to the woman, "You see him right here?" Pointing at me, "Well he ain't shit, and I definitely ain't shit. So, as you can see we're just two pieces of shit sitting in first class." He gives her a big smile and a thumb up.

Shaking my head laughing, "Man, leave them folks alone."

G leans over towards me, "Them niggas at Howard must really like yo ole broke ass to upgrade them cheap ass tickets you bought." Laughing, we put on our headphones, sat back ready to enjoy the flight.

We land probably about 12:00 pm eastern time, getting off the plane and heading down to baggage claims to grab our suitcases. Casually walking through the airport on our way to catch a taxi, G points out a guy holding a sign with my name on it. "Aye! Check that shit out Zeke. You got a limo outside waiting on us?"

Approaching the man slowly, checking all the other people walking around in case somebody else name is Ezekiel Miller. "What's up, I'm Ezekiel Miller, but I didn't ask for a limo." He says his dispatcher told him to be here, so he's here. G walks up behind me, I ask him if he did this since he's always pulling up in a limo.

"Nah, this one ain't on me. But fuck it let's go College Boy." Smacking my butt, he says, "Tighten up pop tart, it's your time to shine."

Startled, "Aye man, don't ever do that shit again. I ain't with that funny shit negro." Loading up the limo we head towards the Holiday Inn. Dozing off for much of the ride, I wake up to the driver turning into the Jefferson Hotel. Immediately I tell the driver he got us in the wrong location. "Excuse me, but we're not staying here. We have reservations at the Holiday Inn over in College Park." The Jefferson Hotel is not a cheap hotel, it cost about five-hundred dollars a night for a single room, I know for damn sure I don't have that type of bread.

But again, the driver says, "Sir, I'm just doing what I'm told. I apologize if you were not informed of the changes to your reservations."

G says to me, "Man, look, just go with the flow and stop worrying about every goddamn thing. Apparently," G says as he's removing his jacket, "Somebody wants us to have a good time, and we need to make sure we have a fucking great time. Stop over analyzing shit for once in your life. We're here my nigga!" I guess he's right. I have been speaking with a couple of fraternities from Howard the last few weeks. They have been trying to sell me on why I should pledge with them, so it's possible any one of them could have made these changes. Still, a little concerned about us having reservations. I tell the driver not to leave until we wave him off.

G and I walk up to the check-in counter with our suitcases, I give them my info and

right away an Asian guy came from the back
and says, "Right this way Mr. Miller." I go
to wave the driver off, but he was already
gone. The bellhop kid and the Hotel Manager
escorts us to the top floor. Stepping out of
the elevator and right into a penthouse
suite overseeing downtown DC. The manager
hands me his card and tells me if anything
is needed to call him personally. Slowly
walking toward the center of the room
looking around. There's a bar at one end of
the room and a jacuzzi at the other end.
There's a 52-inch TV with a PS4, and an Xbox
One hooked up with a bunch of games. G looks
at me, and with such excitement in his
voice, "Yeah College Boy, you finally made
it. Let's hurry the fuck up and handle this
school shit so we can chase after these
hoes." I send Alexis a text letting her know
I landed. Waiting for a response from her,
but after a few minutes, I didn't get one.
Fuck it! I can't make a motherfucker like
me. Hopping in the shower, so I can to

freshen up and go handle this school business.

Howard University, wow, it's a surreal feeling. So many famous African American men and women earned their degrees here. People like Roberta Flack, Edward Brooke, Thurgood Thomas, all walked through these same prestigious doors. I feel honor to be able to attend an HBCU that is enriched with so much history. Howard University received their charter March 2nd, 1867 and is considered the capstone of the Afro-American educational experience in America. Named after Oliver Otis Howard, a Civil War general. There is no doubt that Howard University is where I need to be. During the registration process, I'm meeting a lot of cool people. The staff and everybody I've encountered is super friendly, most of them know who I am because when you're getting a full ride, and a chance to make history, your name tends to be mention in many conversations. A meeting is set up for me to meet with Omega Psi Phi. The Ques! I have every desire to pledge to a fraternity once school starts. The Ques is on the top of my list of fellowships. When I first came for a campus tour, I met with a bunch of the Big Brothers from Omega Psi Phi, but this time around I'm meeting with Vice Basileus of the Omega Psi Phi. Making sure to thank him for everything they've done for me up to this point. I wish I could stay and chat with the Ques longer, but with so many things to take care of there's no way possible. The short time we conversed for was very constructive and informative.

Crossing through campus to get to the gym to meet Coach Davis. This is a meeting I've been looking forward to. He has chairs set up in the middle of the basketball court. Coach and I shake hands as I introduce him to G. Coach Davis has been in steady contact with me and my Mom ever since I committed to Howard. He reminds me of my Dad a little bit. So, whenever he speaks, I take it to heart. "I'm glad you're here Zeke, I know you had a lot of other options,

Ali Shakur

but I'm thrilled you chose us as your new home. In life, there are a lot of temptations, and once you get here, the temptations will increase. Even though we hold all our students to a high standard, there are some that just, have their own way of doing things. I can't tell you who to hang with or who not to hang with. All I ask of you is not to lose focus on what's important to you. Don't let those outside forces dictate the choices you make. You're in a real position to do great things, and I'm here to help guide you. When the school year starts, and the season gets going, I need you to be the leader you're born to be. Not just on the court or in class, but in life as well." Coach tells me that I'm not guaranteed a starting spot, but anything can happen between now and the opening tip-off.

Extending my hand to shake Coach's hand as the meeting is wrapping up. "I'm just excited to be playing at a collegiate level. To even have made it this far only inspires me to go further. I look forward to representing Howard University."

G starts mumbling shit under his breath, which causes Coach to address the issue, "Is there something you want to say, young man?"

G stands up knocking his chair over, "You know what bothers me? I've known this nigga my whole life, I've watched Zeke become the best hooper to ever come out of Illinois. They retired his high school jersey, and for you not to be able to guarantee him a starting spot is bullshit."

Coach lets out a quick laugh. I'm sorry you feel he deserve a starting spot, but nothing is given on this team. You got to earn everything, I'm sure Zeke knows that. I can tell you're a good..."

G interrupts, "You can't tell shit, cause if you could, you would be guaranteeing him a starting role! Man, I'm out, fuck him and all that bullshit he's talking about." G storms out the gym. I apologize to Coach for the outburst.

Coach responds with a look of concern.
"Zeke be careful out there, I would hate for
you to lose everything you worked hard for.
Friends or not, don't allow yourself to be
steered in the wrong direction."

Excusing myself to catch up with G in
the hallway. I'm fucking pissed off, and if
I weren't in this school hallway, I'd punch
him dead in his fucking eye. "Nigga! What
the fuck was that all about?" G tries to
brush it off and walk away.
Grabbing him by the shoulder and turning him
around, "Nigga don't turn your back on me!"

He pushes me back away from him. "That
nigga ain't trying to give you the respect
you earned on the court. I'm the Sports
Agent here and I call a flag on the fucking
play. He needs to worship the court you play
on."

"I feel you, but you can't be
disrespecting motherfuckers because you
disagree with them. That shit is going to
give our brand and us a bad reputation.
Nigga, like straight up, if you weren't my

fucking homeboy I'd fuck you up, that was
some hoe shit you did back in there. This is
our fucking future you're playing with. You
need to get it together G."

"First off, you wouldn't fuck up shit.
But whatever, my bad Zeke, maybe I shouldn't
have been a dick about it. But either way,
he needs to know that when you step on the
court, everything needs to revolve around
you! Not them fucking scrubs he got running
plays now if yawl trying to win."

"No shit, you think? But on the real, I
believe Coach is looking out for my best
interest, I believe in his principles.
That's why I'm here!"

G shakes his head, "Yeah whatever
nigga. I'm done talking about this
bullshit."

"What the fuck you mean? You started
all this bullshit, and now it's over because
you are done talking about it?"

G smiles, puts his arm around my
shoulder, "Calm down Zeke. You see them,
bitches, over there?" nodding his head in

their direction, "I want the thick light skin one with the big titties, and you can have the little skinny bitch with the bubble booty." G pimp walks over to the females, who stood listening to us argue. The girls are giggling, he approaches and asks the skinny girl what's so funny?

She replies, "We heard yawl over there having a lover's quarrel." Both women start laughing.

G smacks his lips, "Nah baby, that's my homeboy Zeke, he's about to take yawl basketball team to new heights." I walk over once I see G pointing at me. "Ladies this is Ezekiel Miller aka Zeke, and I'm G, the genius marketing mastermind slash sports agent." He extends his hand in an attempt to have them introduce themselves. Amused, the thick girl says her name is Tanya, and her friend name is Bre. "It's truly a pleasure to meet you!" G says kissing both their hands.

Bre, holding her books close to her chest laughs, "Girl, he thinks he's Romeo!"

95

"He's cute though!" Tanya says as she bumps her hip against G winking at him.

G, rubbing his hands across his hair waves, "So what yawl bout to do right now? We're staying over at the Jefferson hotel. Yawl should come through."

"Yeah right! Ain't no easy targets this way," Bre says rolling her eyes at G.

Jumping into the conversation to save G from pissing them off. "He didn't mean it like that, we came out here from Illinois for registration, but now that shit is done, we just trying to find something to do." They agree to kick it with us but needs to handle other business first. They tell us to meet them near the White House in a couple hours. We rush to the room to change our clothes to go meet up with Tanya and Bre. Walking around DC checking out some of the historical monuments, the energy is fantastic, Tanya and Bre are cool as hell. Standing at the Martin Luther King Jr. Memorial, making plans for later tonight.

Ali Shakur

G gets a phone call, he answers in a low tone voice like he's trying to keep the call a secret. He looks at me for a minute and walks away to talk. The girls and I stand around the memorial, taking pictures, laughing and joking around. I peep G from a distance, unable to make out what he was saying, but there's laughter involved. I go back to playing around with Tanya and Bre. G quietly walks up, he stands looking at me with a smirk on his face and his phone to his ear, "Yeah, I'm keeping everything together. Yep, he really is doing this school thing. Why wouldn't he? Ok, cool… See you soon, peace." He puts his phone away.

"What was that about?" I ask him. "Damn nigga! Why you all in my business? Sometimes I wonder about you Zeke! I think you want to give me that ass, but I don't know if you can handle this full force." He grins walking towards Bre and Tanya, he puts his arms around both of them, and starts walking off towards the Lincoln Memorial.

We stay out with Bre and Tanya until about 9:00 pm. G tries to convince them to come back to the room, but they decline. We make our way back to our room. Nothing seems to be popping off tonight, so we're sitting in the hotel room chilling and bullshitting on social media when I figure now would be the perfect time to see what's been up with him. "G, do you feel some type of way about me going away to school?" He stretches his arms above his head. Yawning, he says, "Zeke, I ain't trying to talk about this shit. Plus, you wouldn't understand even if I told you."

"If you tell me what's up maybe I would!"

"Zeke … Life is about evolving. You're evolving into a great man, and you're already a great basketball player. I just want to be great at something." Trying to be encouraging I tell G to just come to DC with me as we planned since I got accepted into Howard.

"Look G, we can get a nice apartment off campus. While I'm at school, you could be out building our brand or taking some marketing classes. The world is bigger than what's back home." Walking over to the large window overlooking DC, staring out at the White House. "We've always talked about leaving Lake Shore whenever the opportunity came. And now that it's here, you're acting like you don't want to leave! G, the world is ours for the taking, so let's take that shit."

G walks up next to me, puts his arm on my shoulder, "That's the plan Zeke… That's the plan."

Unforgiven

"I am GOD! I give life, and I take life!"

Making it home Sunday about 3:00 pm.
After a short weekend, I just need to get in
my bed and relax. The whole time I was in DC
I didn't hear from Alexis at all, I'm
disappointed, but I'm not going to let it
get me down. Turning the knob to the front
door and stepping into the house. My heart
starts beating out my chest, I get this
feeling like someone kicked me in my
stomach. Shock, fear, confusion, anger all
hit me at once. I watch my Mom and Hugo
dance around the front room to salsa music
sharing laughs together. I stand, not saying
anything, just watching, and they don't even
notice me standing here. Not until Hugo spun
my Mom around and she catches a glimpse of
me. She runs up giving me a hug, but my eyes
are locked on Hugo. He's still dancing with
this sadistic smile. Dropping my suitcase on
the floor, I ask my Mom what was going on.

Hugo steps up, my Mom introduces him as
Special Agent Luis Santiago with the FBI.

She can tell I'm frightened. "Are you ok Zeke?" Still not taking my eyes off Hugo, I say yes. Hugo extends his hand for me to shake it. I don't move, there is no attempt from me to shake his hand. "Zeke," my Mom says with cheerfulness in her voice. "Agent Louis wanted to stop by to inform us that JD murder is solved and you're no longer a suspect."

My voice thick with emotion, "I didn't know I was even a suspect." What the fuck is going on right now? Thoughts are racing through my head. Was Agent Sanchez and Agent Thomas really FBI Agents? Or are they just agents for Hugo?

My Mom grabs my suitcase, "I guess you would like to talk with Zeke, so I'll leave you two alone." My Mom gives Hugo a hug, "Thank you for stopping by." She disappears up the stairs. Hugo slowly walks closer to me, grinning, "Your Mom is a very lovely woman."

Stepping back, "I don't want to hear that shit. What the hell are you doing here?"

He moves towards the couch to sit down. Crossing his legs, he lights a cigar, "I hope you enjoyed your trip to DC."

I don't understand why he cares, but I entertain the question by saying yes. "Good! Very good my friend. I hope you appreciate all that I provided for you?"

Confused I ask what was that he provided? He ashes his cigar on the floor.

"Don't play stupid my friend." I move slowly away from the stairs and to the chair near the kitchen entrance, thoroughly uneasy.

"The first-class plane tickets, the limos, the hotel suite, all that, was you?"

Hugo stands up, grabs his jacket off the coat rack. He turns to me, "I told you we're family and my family is treated like royalty." He pulls out a rubber band full of money and tries to give it to me.

Putting my hands up, "I don't want anything from you!" His jaws tighten, he blows smoke from his nose, and drops the money on the floor, then walks out the front door. Letting out a sigh of frustration, I don't think my life will ever be the same again. I imagined Hugo was long gone, but he's been here the whole time.

Quickly running upstairs to my room to call G, but he doesn't answer. Pacing back and forth in my room trying to figure out a way to get away from this dude. Only a few weeks left before I leave for school and this nigga shows up at my house pretending to be with the FBI, dancing with his fucking hands around my mother's waist. Slamming my fist down on my desk. Ugh! Who the fuck can I turn to for help? Telling my Mom what's up is out the question, she's already been manipulated by him. JD is gone and G is dealing with whatever issues he got. Trusting the Feds is a risky move that I'm not willing to take. There's no way of knowing who's on Hugo's payroll and who's not. I just need to navigate through these next few weeks without any other bullshit. Then I'm out of Lake Shore for good.

The following day around noon, I get a text from Bear telling me to come outside. Stepping out the front gate, I see G coming down the street, we both hop in the truck and take off. Walking into Hugo's office, it's like deja vu! Hugo's sitting at his desk watching his security monitors. He turns his chair around to face us. With a big smile, the gold around his teeth sparkles, he jumps up with his arms open wide, "Welcome back my friend. I hope your time away from the family was restful because now it's time to get back to work." This time around, Hugo wanted things done differently. Instead of bikes and backpacks and riding through the city, he wants us to manage The Pizza Joint. The same Pizza Joint that pop up a few blocks away from the house. The setup as he tells us is simple. All day long he would have his delivery people delivering pizza orders, which most of the orders would be fake, but that was the cover-up. The Pizza Joint isn't a dine-in place, and the focus is strictly deliveries and carry-outs, so that means customers could only phone in and place orders to have whatever was ordered delivered or picked up. The delivery person would take the food to whatever location that was given over the phone, and when they would return from the delivery, their pizza bag would be filled with money. Delivery to houses are usually real food orders, but deliveries made to businesses or other entities are mostly fake. Some of the workers were coming back with anywhere from seventy-five thousand dollars to five-hundred thousand dollars. For tax purposes, we had to fill out W-4 forms and report in like regular nine to five jobs.

Damn! I thought we were out and away from this dude, but we're now overseeing one of his million dollar operations. One of the things I notice right away is most of the drivers are from the neighborhood. All the drug dealers, or so-called gangsters, male and female, had all come to work for Hugo. One of Hugo's favorite workers happens to be Trays lil brother Ronnie. My curiosity causes me to ask him how he and everybody else ended up working for Hugo. Pulling me to the side as if he was keeping a secret, "Hugo told us he was paying seven hundred dollars a week, plus whatever tips we received if we stay off the street corners and stop fucking up the hood." So, that explains why the neighborhood is changing its appearance. Hugo's putting everybody to work and making sure they get money only through him. The night Hugo introduced us to Fat Tony, I did hear him mention that him and his investors would make millions off the land once it's properly cleansed. He has business partners he wants to please with the product he's producing. Not only was the product drugs, but it's also Lake Shore.

The more I work at The Pizza Joint, the more I see how close Hugo and G have become. Pulling G to the side to ask him what was up with him and Hugo acting like best friends. He rolls his eyes, "Man come on! You about to start tripping!? Hugo is paying us a few G's a month to watch these motherfuckers count money and deliver pizza. I don't know about you, but I'm trying to get paid." Not sure if it's the money or the whole lifestyle that Hugo provides that G is in love with, but I try to reason with him in a way he would understand where I stand.

"G, if we keep working for Hugo, everything we worked for would be for nothing. There is no good ending to this shit G! Come on man think."

G drops his head down. Annoyed, he looks back up at me, shakes his head, quickly steps in my face, with his finger pointing in my chest. "Everything we worked for? Nigga, you mean everything you worked for! You got the scholarship to go play ball, and you want me to follow behind you, you want to dictate my life, my every move. Well, guess what Zeke, I'm not your fucking flunky! I make my own decisions, and if you

can't handle that shit, then you know what?
Fuck you! College Boy." G goes to the back
room where the money is being counted. So,
he does feel some type of way with me going
to school! He must have been harboring his
feelings for a while. If I knew before now,
he was feeling this way I would have done
things differently.

Walking into the money room to try to
talk to G. Without even looking at me, he
says, "Get the fuck out the way!"
Intentionally bumping into me as he walks
past.

A few days go by, and there haven't
been any signs of G. No phone calls, no text
messages. No nothing. We've had our shares
of disagreements, but we always squashed it
before the day ended. But this time, I don't
know, whenever I call his phone it goes
straight to voicemail. He's not coming in to
work, and I have no clue what's going on
with him.

A couple hours after checking into The
Pizza Joint Hugo comes storming in with both

Ali Shakur

Bear and G. They walk past me as if I was
invisible. Bear snatches Ronnie from out the
room. Hugo tells Bear and G to take Ronnie
outside to the alley. Hugo turns to me
pointing his finger, "Follow me." Out in the
alley, Ronnie is taking a brutal beating.
Hugo orders them to stop, I move closer to
G, "What the hell is going on?"

He ignores me. Hugo bends down next to
Ronnie, and one by one he breaks each of his
fingers. Hugo stands, stares down in disgust
at Ronnie's bloody and beaten face. Hugo
removes his shirt displaying his muscle
frame through his wife beater. "Why steal
from me? After I take you off the corner and
put money in your pockets, you still take
from me! If you needed help with finances,
you could've come to me. You were one of my
favorites, but now you disappoint me. Ronnie
manages to get on his knees, begging for
mercy, crying for his life to be spared.
Hugo kicks him back down to the ground. Hugo
looks over his shoulder, he calls on me to
come to him. But I don't move, I'm frozen,

my eyes widen, stuck on Ronnie as he struggles to get up. Hugo turns all the way around, snaps his finger, points down to the ground. "Zeke! Come here! Now!"

I hesitate, but I slowly walk towards him. He's sizing me up, his eyes full of flames. He places both hands on my shoulders, looking me in the eyes. It's hard to make eye contact with him, the evil in his eyes has me trembling with fear. He hands me a gun that Bear passes over to him. In a low soft voice, he says to me, "Kill him!"

Stuttering, "I… I… Hugo I…" Breathing heavy, my eyes water up. I point the gun at Ronnie, he closes his eyes, my finger on the trigger, I never been this scared in my life. My mind blacks out … I hear Hugo whisper, "Kill him."

"I can't do it." I lower the gun, unable to lift my head to face Hugo, my voice cracks, I fight back the tears. "I can't do it… I'm not a killer." Ronnie immediately begins pleading for forgiveness.

Hugo violently slaps Ronnie to the ground. "You want forgiveness? You beg for my mercy? I want you to confess your sins you have committed towards me."

Ronnie gets back on his knees, his hands in a praying manner. "Please Hugo!" Ronnie's face is full of tears. "I was wrong, and I will do whatever I have to do to repay you. Please … Please, Hugo, I'm sorry!" Hugo grabs Ronnie by the neck, his lips draw back in a snarl, Ronnie's face is turning blue from lack of oxygen.

Hugo releases his grip, dropping Ronnie onto his hands and knees. He pats Ronnie on the head. "I forgive you. I forgive you for your sins that you have committed towards me."

Ronnie back on his knees, "Thank you! Oh, God thank you!"

"But I cannot forgive you for your disloyalty." Bang! Hugo shoots Ronnie right between the eyes with a golden design .45 caliber Desert Eagle. Watching in horror as brain matter flows out the back of his head and his body drops, while blood leaks from his head. Hugo kneels next to the body, pulls out a knife, sticks it in the wound. The blood of Ronnie covers the blade. He walks towards me slowly with death in his eyes, he holds the blood soak blade in front of my face. I'm trembling uncontrollably. Taking the tip of the blade, he taps it on my forehead. I feel the blood from the knife drip down my face. Am I next? He closes his eyes, takes a deep breath, "Show me the palms of your hands." My hands shaking uncontrollably, but I do as I'm told. He holds the knife to my face again, using each of my palms he wipes the blade clean. He takes another deep breath, "You now have his blood, on your hands." He walks away, leaving me to stare at my bloody palms. Full of confidence he tells Bear to get everyone to the alley. "I want them to bear witness! I am GOD! I give life, and I take life!" Everyone made their way outside into the alley. A girl screams out and kneels beside Ronnie crying frantically. Unfazed, Hugo proceeds to speak in a dominant voice, "He decided to take fifteen thousand dollars from me. Now here lays this lifeless thief. If you take from me, I will take something that is worth more to you." Hugo looks down at the girl. "Was he your lover?"

Someone says, "No that's her brother."

Hugo stares at her as she cries over the body. He places his hand on her head, rubbing it as if she were his pet. In an almost sympathetic manner, he tells the girl, "I'm sorry for your loss." He gets in the car with Bear and G, and they drive off.

Hours later G comes back with a group of guys to clean up the body. The girl is still outside with her dead brother crying as she holds him. G tells the girl where the body is going, hands her a business card to where she can go pick out a casket for her brother. I wait until G isn't talking to anyone to approach him and apologize for forcing my life on him. "Look G, I should have asked you how you felt about certain things, instead of assuming you would just follow my lead."

"I'm not tripping on that shit anymore. Let's leave the past in the past and continue to work towards the future. But stop treating me like I'm your fucking child Zeke." I ask if he was coming back to manage The Pizza Joint with me, he says no, he's now Hugo's enforcer next to Bear. I can't believe what this nigga is telling me. Concerned about his safety, I say to him, "To be somebody enforcer G, you got to be ready to kill for them or enforce whatever they say with no issue and that ain't you. This is not how you were raised."

He takes a half step back, looks me up and down, shakes his head, with hostility, "There you go, telling me what the fuck I can and can't do. But I guess you just can't help yourself huh? Everything in your little world got to be perfect. But guess what Zeke, it ain't! You're walking around here thinking that scholarship is going to save you. Well, news flash College Boy, ain't no leaving this. Not now it ain't. These motherfuckers got their own set of rules, and it doesn't include walking away to go to college." I try to interrupt him. "No, fuck that Zeke, shut the hell up and listen for once. If you can't get your mind right, you going to end up like that motherfucker outside. You don't have control Zeke, so stop thinking you do, stop thinking of a way out of this! Do what the fuck you got to do for these motherfuckers." He pulls out a gun, "Or you might as well put it to your head and pull the trigger ya damn self." Staring at the gun that's in his hand. My shoulders droop over, I feel lost. I've lost my best friend, and I'm feeling like I'm losing everything I work so hard for. G tucks his gun into his back waistline and leaves with the men he came with.

Sitting at the desk in my room, just thinking about G, Hugo, and how my life was crumbling right before my very eyes, and there was nothing I could do about it. I try to reach out to G but never got a reply. I'm

too nervous to go back to The Pizza Joint
after what happened today. But I know if I
don't go back there's no telling what would
happen. Shit, ain't no telling what will
happen if I do go back. It feels like time
is moving slow. Flashing back to what G said
earlier, "Zeke, you think you're in control,
but you're not. You might as well pull the
trigger ya damn self."

I need to tell somebody about what's
going on, but who? Afraid the consequences
would be dire if I mentioned anything to
anybody. For me to free us from Hugo, I
would really have to submerge myself in his
world and figure a way to bring him down.
Does Hugo even trust me enough to allow me
to get as close to him as I once was?

Later that evening my Mom walks into my
room. She's dress like she's about to hit
the red carpet. "Mom, what the hell? Where
you going dressed like that?"

She smiles, twirling around showing off
her dress, "I take it I'm looking fabulous!"
She sits on the edge of the bed next to me,

116

"Zeke I've been without your father for a few years, and I've met somebody that I think is a pretty cool guy." Not sure what to say; besides, who is he? Just as I finish getting the words out, I jump up in terror! He's here, standing in my bedroom doorway with his evil grin. My Mom looks at me with her happy look, "You remember FBI agent Luis Santiago?" Stepping back, the fear prevents me from speaking, I'm feeling nauseated.

He approaches me, "It's good to see you again. Have you been staying out of trouble? I would hate to get a call about them finding you in an alley." Swallowing hard, my eyes shifts away from him.

My Mom intervenes, "Alley? What do you mean?"

He turns to my mother with a smile and his hand extended, "Shall we?" My Mom gives me a kiss and says not to wait up as she leaves out with Hugo.

Laying in my bed staring up at the ceiling thinking about my Mom. There's a feeling that tells me my Mom isn't in any

immediate danger, he's playing mind games
with me. Could I really leave for school
knowing the Devil is hanging around my Mom?
If it weren't for me, none of this would be
happening. Having no other choice, but to
pull out all my school info, and start to
gather the information I need to resign from
school. G is right, there's no walking away
from this. Not only did I put myself in
danger, but I also put my family in danger
as well. My phone starts vibrating like
crazy, I'm receiving text message after text
message. My Mom is the first thought that
popped into my head. I grab my phone and
begin reading the messages.

It's her! It's Alexis! She finally
reached out to me. I have so many questions
I want to ask her. Why did she leave the way
she did? Where is she? And more importantly,
will I ever see her again? I could tell by
her responses that she was being secretive.
She never says anything about where she is
or why she left. The only straight answer I
get is that she never meant to hurt me. She

promises that once the time is right, we could pick up where we left off. I don't know how I feel about what she's saying. Why isn't the time right now? What is she hiding? I know she's not going to tell me more than what she wants me to know and I don't want to press the issue on anything. Not wanting to lose her again, so I accept what she was willing to give and just take it from there.

I'm just happy we're back communicating. We text one another into the late night until she finally stops replying. It's 3:00 am in the morning when I hear my mother coming upstairs to her room. Stepping out to make sure she was alone, she sees me creeping out my door and ask why I'm still up. "I was worried about you and wasn't going to be able to sleep until you got home. How was your time with Santiago?"

Her face lights up with pleasure. "It was amazing! We enjoyed dinner at a beautiful restaurant where anything I could think of to eat was prepared by a top chef.

We took a horse and carriage through the city and we ended up at some loading dock where there was a helicopter waiting for us. Zeke, this man flew a helicopter through the city. Oh, my god it was so romantic!"

Fuming with anger, almost enough to say fuck it, and tell everything. "Mom, just please be careful. If it's too good to be true, then most likely it isn't true."

She kisses me on the forehead, "Thank you, but I think I can look out for myself Zeke, now go to sleep son."

Still fuming with anger, as I walk into work the next day in a shitty mood. I walk in to see Fat Tony sitting in my office. What the hell? I haven't seen Fat Tony since the first time I met him at Hugo's house. Throwing my keys on the desk and removing my jacket. "What's up, what are you doing here?"

He sits back in the chair, kicks his feet up on the desk, "Apparently, you can't do your job correctly B, so me and my niggas is here to make sure shit doesn't get fucked up again. Na'mean?!"

Looking around, "What you mean your team?"

He gets directly in my face. "Yeah, nigga my team. So, check this shit out B, theses Shore niggas, they finish. If you don't get on board all the way, then yo ass is done too B! I'm Dead ass right now! Niggas is done playing games with you lil niggas. Straight up!" Standing in the doorway watching as Tony sit back down and grab a magazine. He looks up from his magazine, and sees I'm still standing here. "Nigga you still here? Go do some fucking work B, get the fuck outta my face."

I storm out the building slamming the door. Sitting in my truck calling Hugo, he answers the phone, "Yes my son?"

Pissed and not giving a fuck, "Look, I'm not your son and stay the hell away from my Mom."

He laughs, "That may be hard to do considering she loves the way I caress her body."

"Fuck you Hugo, I swear if ..."

He interrupts viciously, "You swear what? You ungrateful little shit. You dare threaten me? I will slice your fucking throat from ear to ear. You think you have heart? I will rip it out of your fucking chest and feed it to your whore mother!" I heard what sounded like him slamming his fist down on a table. "I own you! Your soul belongs to me! Don't you know that Ezekiel Thomas Miller?" Me not responding causes him to get even more upset. "Answer me when I talk to you puto maricon!" Struggling to get the words out, I manage to mumble out a yes. He starts laughing, "Now that we have an understanding, what brings this friendly phone call?"

My mind is entirely blank. There was a moment of silence before I ask, "What's up with Fat Tony and the Black Kings? I thought The Pizza Joint was my thing."

"Ezekiel," Hugo says, speaking more calmly, "Tony and his friends are there for insurance purposes. I can't have people doing whatever they want. My friend, I thought you had everything under control, but unfortunately, I was wrong. Since you allowed street rats to steal from me, I no longer believe you have my best interest at heart. And that my friend is a terrible thing."

Not trying to upset Hugo again, so I choose my words carefully and speak in a low soft tone. "But Hugo, I didn't let him steal anything. I've been loyal to you. I've done everything you ever asked me to do. I have no control over what them niggas did when they were out on the road doing pick-ups and drop-offs. I only saw what they did when they were here." There's silence... Repeatedly I say hello, still no response. I look at my phone, the call had ended. Sitting in my truck staring at The Pizza Joint. Screaming out FUCK! Why me!? What did I do that was so bad in life that caused this to happen to me? Walking back into The Pizza Joint, Tony's in the money room on the phone, watching as the money machines count the money.

As I approach Tony I hear him say, "Don't worry Jefe, we'll take care of it for you."

Curiously I ask, "Take care of what?"

Tony blows cigarette smoke in my face, "Mind your fucking business kid." He walks away and starts talking to one of his Kings that stands at the back door. I notice the guy he was talking to look at me nodding his head in agreement with whatever Tony is telling him.

I stay around the pizza joint even though I feel unwanted. Trying not to cross paths with Tony, but it's not easy. Fuck this shit! Grabbing my stuff and rushing out the door, I'm just going to go home and deal with this shit another day. On my way home, there's a car following me at every turn. Afraid to go straight home, so I'm driving around until I can lose whoever is following me. I try calling G, but no answer. Finally, I get home, and my mother isn't here. Walking into the kitchen, she left me a note on the refrigerator that reads, "Out to dinner be back later. Take the trash out." Before I left this morning, she didn't mention anything about going out. She's probably out with that motherfucker, and it's killing me on the inside. Pacing around the house walking from room to room. I call Alexis in hopes I could see her tonight, her phone rings twice before it goes to voicemail. After about two minutes she calls back.

She's talking as though she's not trying to be heard on the phone. "Hey Zeke, how you been?"

"Lexis I need to see you."

"No Zeke, I can't, right now is not a good time. I can meet you tomorrow."

"Wait! So, your here in Lake Shore? Why you lie and say you were back home?"

She stutters trying to find the answer, "Zeke, I… wait, I'm here, but it's hard to explain. Can you meet me tomorrow?"

Suddenly, I hear a guy's voice in the background, "Who the fuck you on the phone with?" Then the call ends. I should call back, but I don't. What the fuck is going on with Alexis? This shit is bugging me out. I can't even begin to grasp the feeling of emotions that I'm feeling right now. Flopping down on the couch and staring at the black TV screen, just thinking. Sitting in a daze for a while, trying to come up with a conclusion to why Alexis would lie to me. Who was the guy in the background? Was she here in Lake Shore the whole time she was telling me she left to go back home? Jumping up, grabbing the keys to my truck and leaving out to go for a drive to clear my head. I have no idea where I'm going, I'm just driving around the city. Through my rearview, that black Toyota Camry from earlier is following right behind me.

Ali Shakur

It appears to be two males in the front. I speed up, make a quick left heading down 35th. Dam! They're still behind me. The street is empty, no cars in motion and no people out. Fuck it! I increase speed, doing 60 down the one-way street, panicking as both hands griped the steering wheel tightly. The Toyota turns their bright lights on making it hard to see what they're doing through my rear view. Swerving to cut them off, but they managed to pull up. Using my truck to try to ram them off the road, but that only causes me to slightly lose control of my truck.

Rapid fire from a semi-automatic gun

Veering away from the Toyota and... There's screeching from spinning tires. My breathing is heavy… I can't move… My eyes open slowly … Then everything goes black.

No Way Out

"PLEASE GOD, SOMEBODY HELP ME!"

Beeping from a heart monitor

The pain is unbearable, my head is pounding. Trying to sit up, but I can't. What happened? I remember hearing gunshots. Was I shot? Am I dead? A nurse walks in, she's checking my IV fluid, she sees me coherent and says, "Mr. Miller, you are one lucky young man."

Turning slowly, and barely able to speak, "What happened to me?"

She moves around the room checking different machines. "You ran into a light pole at a very high speed. Your vehicle's front end got smashed in severely."

Using the remote on the bed to sit the back of the bed up. "I heard gunshots."

The nurse stood in the doorway, with a pleasant smile. "Yes, your car was shot up, but you managed not to get hit. I'm not sure how that happened, but some officers would like to speak with you." Agent Thomas and Sanchez walk in.

I quickly pretend to be sleep, keeping my eyes open, just enough to see what was going on. Thomas walks to the side of the bed. "Are you fucking kidding me? We just heard you in here talking. Now your ass want to fake like your sleeping." He sticks his finger in my ear, startled I move quickly, yelling in pain from the sudden movement of my body.

Did this nigga just give me a fucking a wet willy? Looking in disgust at Agent Thomas, "Why the fuck is you playing in my ear?"

"Why the fuck you in here acting like you're sleeping?"

Agent Sanchez brings a chair over and sits on the other side of my hospital bed. "Zeke, tell us what happened?"

"I'm not telling you shit!"

Agent Thomas claps his hands together and moves in closer. "Look Zeke, we're trying to help you. We can't help if you're not willing to talk to us."

Trying to sit up, but the pain won't allow me. "You're not trying to help, you're trying to kill me."

Agent Thomas begins laughing, "We're not trying to kill your black ass. Them niggas you got yourself mixed up with is trying to kill you."

"Rolling my head towards Agent Sanchez. "Look, I just need to rest. When I'm ready to talk, I'll call you."

My Mom comes rushing in crying, "Oh god my baby!" She pushes Agent Thomas out the way. "Are you ok? What happened?" Agent Sanchez tells my Mom to call him in the morning. They need to talk to me as soon as possible.

He places his hands on my Mom's shoulder, "We're going to figure this out Mrs. Miller." He motions his head for Agent Thomas to walk out with him. After they clear the room, I tell my Mom that I was driving home, and some car started shooting.

I swerved to get away and ran into a pole. Her face full of tears, shaking her head, distraught. She asks me if this had anything to do with JD.

"I don't think it does, but I don't know. I didn't even see the car, I just heard shots." She sits next to the hospital bed rubbing my hand. Glancing over, I ask if she was with Santiago.

She jerks her head back, shocked that I even ask that question. "No baby, I was with Grandma Belle. We went to bingo and had dinner afterward. I only went out with Louis once. It's something about him that doesn't seem right, I just couldn't figure it out, so I stopped it before it went any further." Looking away staring at the door, for some reason I'm waiting for them to walk through that door and finish the job that they started.

After a while, my Mom dozes off leaving me to watch TV alone. The door began to open slowly, my heart starts to beat faster. Reaching over to wake my Mom, she mumbles

something but doesn't wake up. Closing my
eyes, it'll be all over shortly. The hair on
my neck stands as I can feel the person
standing over me. Deep slow breaths…
Waiting… I feel a finger under my nose, I
slowly open my eyes… What the hell! It's G
standing over me with a big ass smile on his
face. "You alright my nigga?"

"Yeah fool, why you creeping in here?
Putting yo dirty ass finger in my face."

He smacks his lips, "Man I was checking
to see if you were breathing. They be doing
that shit in the movies all the time." I
haven't heard from G in a minute, I know
he's out there with Hugo doing God knows
what.

My Mom finally wakes up and sees G.
"Hey G, how are you?"

She gets up to give him a hug. "I'm
good Mrs. Miller, I just wanted to come
check on this knucklehead, and make sure
he's doing OK." She smiles, leaving to head
down to the cafeteria to get some coffee. As

soon as she walks out the room, G turns to me and asks what happened.

"I think Tony or somebody under him tried to kill me."

"WHAT! That fat fuck! I knew that bitch was on some other shit."

"Yeah well, I believe Hugo gave the order."

"Hugo?" G looks as though he gets a little upset, "Why the fuck would Hugo want to take you out? You ain't even a fucking threat to him or the family." He walks over to the window, he stands glaring out in silence.

"G, look… I can't tell you how to live your life, but I'm done with this shit. I remember you telling me the only way out is death, but I'm not dying. Not yet at least."

G turns around slowly, he looks at the TV for a moment. His phone starts ringing, he looks at it but doesn't answer it. "I'm sorry Zeke, this is all my fault. If I had never agreed to take that book-bag from JD, you wouldn't be here in this situation. I

fucked up, I fucked up big time. I promise
I'll fix everything." He starts walking
towards the door with his head down.

"G!" He stops, he doesn't turn to face
me, he lifts his head to hear what I have to
say. "I love you, my dude, please take care
of yourself." He walks out the door, saying
nothing.

The doctor walks in super early in the
morning. My Mom is awake, but I'm still
sleeping, she whispers in my ear waking me
up so the doctor could tell us what's going
on. The good news is I don't have any broken
bones. I'm basically, just banged up and
bruised pretty bad. A couple days of rest, a
few pain pills and I'll be back on my feet.
The bad news is, I got to go out into the
world not knowing when they'll try to end my
life. The only thing I can do at this point
is to wait and see what happens next.

The doctor signs my release papers, and
about an hour later I'm ready to leave. My
Mom's pushing me through the hospital in a
wheelchair, as we approach the elevator

there's this black guy in all black with his hat down low standing near the elevator. Being cautious, I tell my Mom to use another elevator because this one doesn't lead to the main exit. As we're passing, I'm staring at him, trying to see who he is. He looks up just enough for me to see his eyes and the crown tattoo that's under his eye. He doesn't make any sudden moves, he just grins as I move past him. I'm beginning to get nervous, there is no way I'm getting out of this hospital alive. My Mom is clueless to the danger we're in, I want to tell her, but how? She probably won't even believe me. The elevator door opens, and we get in, the door is about to close, but a hand stops it, and a doctor gets in with a smile. He doesn't push any buttons to a specific floor, he just stands there looking at a clipboard with papers attached.

He places his hand on my shoulder and asks me how I'm feeling. Looking up at him, there it is, a tattoo of a crown under his eye. My heart drops, I jerk my shoulder away from his hand. My Mom looks down at me and asks if I was ok. "Yes ma'am, I'm ok."

"Zeke, you look like you've just seen a ghost," she says looking at me strangely. Trying to speak but I can't find the words. The doctor looks at my Mom and asks if he had her permission to check me out really quick.

She agrees. "No, seriously, I'm ok. Please, just let me go!"

He kneels down and whispers, "I bet you're shitting your pants right now you little bitch. I should kill your ass right now." I'm breathing slowly, I'm breathing heavy, my heart is beating fast, my body temperature is rising. He flicks the side of my head as he stands up with a smile, "He'll be ok for right now." The elevator door opens, and my Mom says thank you to who she thinks is a doctor as we exit out. Looking around in the lobby waiting for someone else to appear. Out the main entrance door, two more Black Kings are standing not too far away. One of the Kings opens his jacket to show me he has a gun on him. Filling up with terror, I look at my Mom, but she didn't notice. The King with the firearm flips his cigarette and starts to follow behind us.

My Mom, pushing me slowly across the street into the parking garage. Looking behind us and they're still following us, closer than they were before, the gun is now in his hand, I see him cock it back as they pick up their speed. "Mom hurry please!"

"Boy hush, I can't push your big ass no faster."

She hits the unlock button on her key ring as we get to her Expedition, looking back again, and they were gone. Not a trace of them in sight. What the hell? My Mom gets me in the truck, she goes around to the trunk to put the wheelchair in. I hear a voice say, "let me help you with that." Turning to look out the rear window and see the two Kings who were just following us. Quickly, I opened the truck door and tried to get out, but I fall to the ground. I yell, "Mom no!" She looks around to the passenger side, sees me on the ground, and rushes over to help me get back in the truck. The two Kings folded up the wheelchair and place it in the trunk, then walked around to help my Mom lift me back in the truck.

Shaking in fear, the guy with the gun leans in to put the seat belt around me. I feel the gun pressing against the side of my stomach. Looking at him dead in his eyes, as he's staring back. They say when you're on the verge of dying, your life begins to flash before your eyes. The guy whispers, "Bang! You're a dead nigga!" He puts the gun away, gets out to shake my Mom's hand. She thanks them both and gets into the truck. The two Kings stand waving and watching as we pull off.

On the ride home, my Mom is talking, but I'm zoning in and out of the conversation. I'm checking the side mirror and every car that passes or pulls up alongside us. I'm nervous, I just want to hurry up and get home, but even being home doesn't ensure my safety. My phone starts to vibrate, reaching into my pocket to get it. I answer it, "Hello?" The voice on the other end gives me butterflies in my stomach. It's a voice I needed to hear.

"Hey Zeke, I heard what happened, are you ok?" The softness and beauty of her tone made me forget about my troubles.

"Yeah, I'm ok, just banged up. How did you hear?"

There's a silence, "Zeke, I need to talk to you face to face. Is it ok if I come by later?"

"Yeah, sure. I'll be home in a few minutes. What time you plan on coming over?" She quickly says I'll text you and hangs up.

"Was that her?" My Mom asks as we pull into our driveway.

"Yeah, but Mom I don't know, something ain't right. I mean I really like her, but she's hiding something, and it's bothering me."

"If you're unsure about her, then don't put yourself out there until you feel she's

ready, to be honest and upfront with you."
My Mom gets out the truck and comes around
to help me get into the house and onto the
couch. I text G to tell him I was home, even
though I don't expect him to text me back, I
still need him to know, just because. Still
dealing with pain, I manage to shower and
put on some sweats and a tee shirt. Laid out
on my bed watching old reruns of Martin.
Constantly checking my phone in hopes Alexis
will hit me up soon. 10:00 pm came and still
no text or call from her. I've given up
hope, if she were going to call she would
have done so by now.

Closing my eyes to get some rest, and
placing my phone on my chest, just in case
she did decide to call me. An hour or so
later, I receive a text message. Struggling
to sit up to read the text, thinking it was
from Alexis, but it's not. "You're a dead
man walking." Staring at the text fearful of
what was going to happen in the next coming
days. I wait about thirty minutes before I
try to call the number that sent the text.

The phone rings once, then I got the busy
signal. I stay up most of the night thinking
about death, heaven, and hell. There's no
doubt, I'm going to die soon, but would it
be a slow death full of pain or would I go
fast and peacefully.

A few days' pass, feeling slightly
better, the pain is not as severe, but I
still move slowly. I've been in the house
the whole time since leaving the hospital,
not leaving out for anything. I could have
died three times at the hospital, so I can
only imagine how easy it would be if I were
out and about. G texted me a couple times to
make sure I was ok, but I haven't seen him
since he left the hospital. Alexis is always
in my thoughts, I can't understand how we go
from being damn near in love, to her
becoming a big mystery. I want to give up on
her, but something inside of me won't let me
do it. As far as me going to school, that
shit is out the question right now. They're
not going to let me leave. I know as soon as
I step out my house for longer than a couple

hours, there won't be any making it back home. I don't want my Mom worrying, so I act like everything is ok, even though death is knocking on the front door. What the fuck did I do to make Hugo so mad? Maybe if I call and talk to him, I can find out what I've done and convince him to call off the Kings.

My Mom is planning on going out to play bingo, so I'm going to lay around in my room until it's time for her to leave with Grandma Belle before I call Hugo. I slowly begin dialing his number, my handshaking with every number push. I'm terrified, I haven't spoken with him since I last called him at The Pizza Joint. He answers, "You finally decided to call. I've waited a long time for you. I hear you had an accident."

Speaking in a low tone, "You know what happened. It was your call, but what did I do? What did I do that was so bad to make you want me dead?" There is a silence on the phone for what seems like thirty seconds. "Hello? …. Hugo?"

"Ezekiel, I treated you like my son. I gave you everything you wanted, and you allow some street trash to steal from me. Loyalty, that's all I ever ask of you." I try to convince Hugo that I didn't know the guy was stealing from him, but he's not trying to hear what I have to say. "From day one Ezekiel, you were never willing to commit yourself to being part of my family. You wanted to use me for your personal gain. You thought you were going to get my money and walk away." I try to speak, but he raises his voice in anger. "Do I look like a bitch!? Did you really think I was going to bend over and let you fuck me and then watch as you go off to school, your little black bastard?"

"But Hugo, I tried to tell you I didn't want anything to do with this, but you told me it wouldn't interfere with me going to school."

"The Feds? You didn't think to tell me about the FBI coming to speak with you?" I stutter trying to get the words out, but no matter what I say, I know his mind is already made up, and I need to accept my fate. I hear G talking in the background, it sends chills down my spine. Hugo starts talking to G in Spanish, I'm unable to hear if G is speaking in Spanish or English. Hugo speaking calmly says to me, "This call is finished, my friend." After he hangs up, I start to text G to ask him to help me, but I stop mid-text. What could he do? G is probably just as scared as I am. In frustration, throwing the TV remote control at the wall breaking it into pieces. I lay on the couch with tears coming down my eyes. I cry out; "PLEASE GOD, SOMEBODY HELP ME! I DON'T WANT TO DIE!"

Waking up the following day, there are two missed calls from unknown numbers. I'm not even surprised anymore, I been getting death threats ever since I left the hospital. My Mom asked if I want to go out to breakfast, but I refuse. I just can't bring myself to walk out this house knowing what is waiting for me.

Days and nights went by, and I'm still locked in the house moping around. My Mom is starting to worry about me and insist that I go talk to a counselor since I won't speak to her. She knows something is up, but until I can figure things out, maybe figure out a way out of this shit, I don't plan on talking to anybody. I just want to stay in the house as long as possible. It's only so long I can avoid the inevitable.

"Zeke… Zeke… Wake up! That girl is here." Not sure what she's talking about.

Wiping my eyes, "What girl? What are you talking about?" Squinting my eyes, I look at the time, and it reads 10:23am. Rubbing my eyes again, I see her standing in my room. I get up with mixed emotions. I'm in shock that she's really here. I haven't seen Alexis since I left to go to DC. My Mom gives her a hug and leaves out the room closing the door behind her.

She sits on the bed next to me. "Hey Zeke, I can't stay long, but I needed to see you. I really miss you."

145

My voice raspy, I crack a smile, "I missed you too, more than I can tell you. I'm happy that you're here." Putting my hand over my mouth, because my breath is funky, I ask if she got a minute for me to go freshen up. She shakes her head yes. Literally, I run to the bathroom tripping over my own feet. I hurry up, wash my face, brush my teeth, and rush back to the room.

Alexis is on the phone, she puts her finger to her lips for me to be quiet. Whoever she's on the phone with is asking her a ton of questions. She tells whoever she's talking to that she's at LaToya's house. I can hear the person on the other end yelling at her, she's apparently upset. "Ok, you don't have to yell. I'm sorry! Ok?!? I'm sorry. NO! You don't have to come pick me up. I'm heading to the bus stop now. I'll be back in less than an hour." She hangs the phone up, looks down at the floor, and a tear drops from her face.

Moving in closer to her, "Alexis, please tell me what's going on." She lays her head on my shoulder, sobbing. Wrapping my arm around her, "Alexis, if you're in trouble, just tell me, I can help you.

She quickly lifts her head to look at me. Wiping her tears away, "Really Zeke! You can't even help yourself, how in the hell are you going to help me?"

"Wait?! What the hell is that supposed to mean?"

She grabs her purse, "Nothing Zeke, look I'm sorry, but I have to go. When I get a chance, I'll reach out to you. Just, please try to be safe." I'm not going to let her walk out my door without knowing what the fuck is going on with her. I tell her that I'm walking with her to the bus stop. She refuses and tells me that it's not a good idea, but no matter what she says, she wasn't just going to walk out on me again without some type of explanation.

Walking outside for the first time since leaving the hospital. The brightness of the sun forces me to close my eyes. Putting my hands over my eyes until they can adjust to the intensity of the sun. Taking a deep breath and walking down the porch, Alexis doesn't know I'm putting my life on the line for her, but I love her, I need to know what is going on. "Alexis, can you please slow down and talk to me?" I'm limping trying to catch up with her.

She looks back at me with sadness on her face, "Why are you following me? You need to go back home. If I'm seen with you, it won't be a good thing." I ask her if it was somebody else, she said it wasn't. "You don't understand Zeke, and I just can't." She's shaking her head no, again the tears begin to fall. She stops and hugs me tightly with a kiss. The softness of her lips, the scent of her perfume causes me to grab her by her hips and pull her body closer to my body. She gently pushes me away, she moves her hair behind her ear, and with a smile, she says she loves me, I tell I love her too. Placing her hand on my chest, she says, "This is as far as we can go." She walks away towards the bus stop. I stand watching her, not caring if bullets began to rip through my body, because at this point, my only concern is her.

A white van comes zipping around the corner, two men jump out. Putting my hands to my mouth, I yell out, "ALEXIS!" I try running down towards her, but they quickly throw her in the van, tires screeching as the van busts a U-turn heading back in the direction they just came from. By the time I get to the corner, the van was nowhere to be seen. She dropped her purse, picking it up, I go through it looking for anything that could help me figure out what was going on. The only thing she has in it is her phone and her State ID. Her ID! Racing back home, I'm starting to put two and two together. I know what the fuck is going on and I need to handle this business. I know exactly what I need to do, I just hope it all works out.

Rushing into the house out of breath, my Mom was in the kitchen. She comes out when she hears me stumble in." Zeke, you alright?"

"Yeah, everything is cool." I'm flipping the couch seats, looking for Agent Sanchez's business card. Moving from room to room looking anywhere I think the card may be at. I go upstairs to my room and start throwing shit around looking for his card.

My Mom yells from the bottom of the stairs, "Zeke! Get your ass down here right now!" Shouting from my room, I ask where she put Agent Sanchez's card at.

"It's in my purse, but you need to come down and tell me what's going on. I know something is wrong and you need to tell me."

Slowly coming down the stairs, my Mom is sitting in her chair going through her purse, she hands me the card. "Zeke, don't bullshit me. I want to know what the hell is going on." Taking a deep breath, I take a seat on the couch. Pulling my phone out to send a text to Bear. Looking up at my Mom, she's leaning forward in her chair, her hands together as if she's praying, she's shaking her leg up and down nervously.

Ali Shakur

Gathering up my thoughts, I exhale
blowing my cheeks out. "Ok, a few months
ago, JD asked me and G to do him a favor and
take a book-bag over to this guy. The guy
gave us money, and almost every day after
that we would go pick up book-bags from
around the city and bring it to him, and he
would pay us."

"What was in the bag Zeke?" She stands
up, pacing back and forth in the living
room.

"I don't know for sure, we weren't
allowed to look in the bags. But I know for
a fact it was either drugs, money, or maybe
even both."

She stops pacing, she stands in front
of me. Looking pissed off, she looks as
though she's ready to punch me.

"Boy, you mean to tell me, your black
ass was out there selling drugs? I should
knock your tall, lanky ass out right now!
Zeke, you're a damn idiot. What the fuck
possessed you to do something so fucking
stupid!? You must want to ruin your life?

151

Is that why them Negros was shooting at you? Gosh I can't believe your dumbass right now!"

"Mom, just listen, ok? I didn't want anything to do with it, but I didn't have a choice. I couldn't leave G alone in the mix with the guy, and the reason why they're trying to kill me is because I'm trying to get away from him and he thinks I'm going to tell the police."

She comes and takes a seat next to me, she holds both of my hands. "Who is this guy? Maybe I can talk to him or have …

"Mom no! There is no talking to this guy, I already tried."

"Well, who is he?" I really don't want to tell her who he is, there is a good chance she's going to call him, and make shit even more fucked up, but I've come this far, so I might as well tell her everything.

Standing up, putting my hands behind my head and looking up at the ceiling, I look her in her eyes, "Luis Santiago."

She frowns, "Luis, what do you mean?"

"Luis is not with the FBI. His real name is Hugo."

She starts biting her nails, panicking. "Hugo," she repeats his name a couple times as if she was trying to remember something. She jumps off the couch, her face turns pale. "HUGO! Oh, my GOD! Have you talked to G?"

"No, not since the hospital, I mean a couple text messages here and there. I don't know but he's different, he's probably with them right now." Now I'm confused, my Mom knows something, and she's keeping information from me. She quickly goes into the kitchen and grabs her phone. "Mom, is there something you want to tell me?"

She's panicking, walking back and forth between the living room and the kitchen. I hear her talking on her phone, and I try to eavesdrop, but Bear texts me to tell me he is outside waiting. I leave my phone on the coffee table and grab Alexis's phone. Taking another look at my Mom, I whisper, "I love you!" before walking out the door.

Loyalty

"I'm sorry Zeke, but life is about evolving."

Sitting in the back of the truck staring out the window as Bear drove me to what I know will be my final destination. There is no way I'm making it back home, I regret leaving without giving my Mom a hug or something, but I gotta do what I gotta do. If I told her I was leaving it would have caused a scene, so maybe it was a good thing that I walked out without saying anything. Staring out the window as we drive through Lake Shore; the day is beautiful and sunny. Rolling my window down to enjoy the last moments of my city. The smell of BBQ fills the air, the laughter of the kids running through the water of popped fire hydrants, music is bumping loudly from cars and backyards. A few months ago, I never thought I would be in a fight for my life, but here I am, heading to confront the Devil in hopes I can reclaim my soul.

Feeling emotional and wanting to cry, I manage to hold back my tears, refusing to show signs of weakness. So many things are going on in my head, What the hell does my Mom know about Hugo? Who was she on the phone with? Was it Hugo? I fucked up telling my Mom about Hugo, he probably got one of them Kings heading over to do only God knows what. Who could I blame for this bullshit other than myself? I'm the reason for all this madness, and I just hope he at least spares her life and leaves my body somewhere I can be found.

Bear jumps onto the highway, one of the signs reads Highway 290 North. Breadcrumbs! I just need to keep seeing signs. Not sure where I'm being driven to, but I do remember Hugo talking about having a boat warehouse on Lake Michigan, a little over thirty minutes outside of Lake Shore. Maybe that's where Bear is taking me? Will G be there? Will Hugo kill us both or just me? What will G do? So many thoughts are going through my mind. Alexis… Where is she? Is she safe? I start looking through her phone, reading her text messages, checking her Facebook page and anything else trying to find something that could help. Looking up from the phone, I catch a glimpse of Bear looking at me through the rear view. In a soft almost sad voice, I ask Bear how he hooked up with Hugo. He glances at me through the rearview mirror, his eyes are hidden by the dark sunglasses.

I waited, in hopes he would say something, but he doesn't. Back to staring out the window, I begin talking to Bear, even though I know he's not going to talk back. "Bear? I never wanted to work for Hugo, I just got wrap up in the money, the cars, and women. If I could go back and redo everything I would. Opening Pandora's Box is the biggest mistake I ever made, but I'm just a kid, a kid who was manipulated and now I've ruined my life and everybody's life around me. Bear, I don't know how you got involved with Hugo, but this, this is not how I pictured my life. I'm scared, and I'm just praying this is just a bad dream."

In his thick, raspy voice Bear says, "Everything has an end." Caught off guard by him talking I turn my head waiting for him to say more. He turns the truck onto a rocky road, in the distance I can see a warehouse sitting along Lake Michigan. My fear intensifies, my heart is beating out of my chest. Grabbing the passenger seat and pulling myself closer to the front to get a better look out the front windshield.

I swallow nervously, "So this is it huh?" I ask Bear in hopes I could get some type of clarity. He pulls up close to the building and puts the truck in park. Sitting back, I'm staring at the building through the front windshield. Bear turns around to look at me and tells me to get out. Before I close the door shut Bear says, "Zeke! I'll see you on the other side."

Confused, I lean back into the truck, "Bear, what the fuck does that mean?"

"It means to close the damn door." Slamming the door shut, I head into the building.

As soon as I make it on the inside of the building, I'm met by Fat Tony and Lil Dan, the King that pretended to be a doctor at the hospital. Tony pushes me against a wall and tells Lil Dan to search me for weapons. Looking over my shoulder at Fat Tony, "I don't have any weapons!"

"Shut up bitch! I should put a bullet in yo head right now bitch!" After Lil Dan clears me, Tony grabs me by the shirt and forcefully pushes me to walk ahead of them. I saunter towards a desk that was set up in the middle of the warehouse. Looking around trying to see if there is anybody else here. Hugo comes walking out of an upstairs office wearing a black suit and puffing on a cigar.

He approaches the desk removing his suit jacket, placing it on the back of the chair, he rolls up his sleeves revealing his lion tattoo-covered forearms. Not blinking once since I laid eyes on him, my mouth is dry, I can feel my heart in my throat. He stands, staring into my eyes. Waiting for him to speak, I'm expecting for Tony to

158

shoot me in the back of the head. I wait… I wait… Finally, Hugo walks over to me, my eyes wide, the fear is evident. "Todo lo que quería era lealtad. All I wanted from you was loyalty."

"Wait, Hugo, listen please!" Out of nowhere, Hugo smacks me with his backhand. The force of the hit makes my head turn away, losing my footing and stumbling back into Tony.

Tony pushes me on the ground kicking me in my back. Yelling in pain, "AHHHHH!" Tony and Lil Dan start kicking and punching me, I curl up in the fetal position trying to protect my face and head. The blows feel like I'm being hit with bricks. Stumps to the back of my head, my side, punches to my face. The beating is vicious, losing consciousness for a brief moment, I faintly hear Hugo telling them enough. Laying on the ground barely able to move, this pain is indescribable. Why doesn't he just kill me?

Hugo kneels down, he puts the hot, burning, lit cigar under my chin, the smell of my burning flesh fills my nose. Why doesn't he just kill me? He stands, I manage to roll over onto my back, Hugo tells Tony to get me up and sit me down in the chair. I make my body go limp, so it's tough for them to pick me up. Tony, grabs me by the neck, choking me, "Stand your bitch ass up nigga!" He slams me down in the chair. Hugo grabs me by the chin, making a point to stick his finger where the burning of my flesh is still smoking, he lifts my head up. One of my eyes is swollen shut, I can taste the blood in my mouth. Shaking, scared of whatever torture tactic was next. Hugo, holding my head up by my chin, "Ezekiel, it's unfortunate that you'll never make it to college."

With every ounce of courage I can find, I spat right in his face. "Fuck you, you banana boat motherfucker." The force of a punch to the side of my head knocks me to the ground, my head slams on the concrete. I'm fading out.

My eye slowly opens, and then closes, slightly opens again as I begin to regain consciousness. There are more people standing around. I should just lay here and play dead, I have nothing left in me. Hugo's laughing, the phone in my pocket starts ringing, somebody hands are going through my pockets. Trying to crawl away, Tony stumps on my hands, then kicks me in the ribs. "What the fuck are you doing with my sister's phone nigga?" He kicks me again. "You the bitch nigga my sister been sneaking out seeing?" Tony lands another punch to the side of my mouth. "Get him up!"

Back in the chair, I'm dazed and confused, looking around until Tony is in my eyesight. Spitting out a couple teeth as well as blood, I ask, "Where the fuck is she?"

Tony, ready to land another blow to my face, is stopped by Hugo. "Tony! That's enough." Hugo pulls out his phone and makes a call. Two blurry figures are slowly approaching.

I hear the cries of Alexis, she runs
and kneels at my knees crying
uncontrollably. She lifts my head, "Zeke?"
She screams, "What did you do to him? Just
leave him alone! Please! Zeke, can you hear
me?" Fat Tony grabs her by the hair and
lifts her up. She's screaming trying to
fight him off, he muffs her to the ground.

Tony is furious about finding out that
I been seeing his sister. "You fucking cunt!
You're a whore just like your crackhead
mama. If you weren't my sister, I'd blow
your fucking head off." Hugo tells Tony to
calm down as he moves closer towards G.
Unable to see clearly, it seems as though G
may be in tears, he stands locking eyes with
me, shaking his head in disbelief. Hugo
hands G a .45 caliber Desert Eagle, the same
gun Hugo used to kill Ronnie. Hugo places
his arm around G, and speaks to him in a way
that I never heard him speak to anybody
else. His voice is fill with compassion, "My
son, you know what to do. Just as you
protected your father from JD, just like you

protected my assets from Tray and those street roaches, you must now protect me from Ezekiel. He wants to separate you from me, just as your mother did."

I mumble, "G, please… Help."

A tear drops from his face, he raises the gun, pointing it directly at me. Closing my eye, G says as his voice trembles, "I'm sorry Zeke, but life is about evolving. I hope you find it in your heart to forgive me Zeke."

Bang… Bang… Bang… Bang

Death, the bullets don't feel as I thought they would. No pain, no burning sensation. The bullets must have rip through my body, killing me on impact. The screams of Alexis are loud. Wait? … I'm not dead! I open my eye to see smoke from the barrel of the gun. Looking over to my left and my right, Fat Tony lays on the ground clutching his stomach, trying to crawl away, Lil Dan and another King lay dead on the ground. Hugo, stands unfazed by the unpredictable actions of G. He lights his cigar, "I didn't like that fat maricón anyway. My son, don't disappoint me."

G moves towards me with the gun still in hand. Tapping the top of my head with the handle of the gun, "Zeke, you alright? I mean, I know you're not alright, they did beat your ass pretty bad, but you're still breathing, so that's a good thing, right?"

Blood dripping from my mouth, I mumble the words, "My nigga."

"Damn! They knocked yo fucking teeth out too? You ain't getting no pussy in college with no teeth my nigga! Straight up!" Looking at G for clarification, "G, that's your dad?" "Yeah! That nigga is my Pops! Crazy, right? Apparently, he's the nigga who wrote that letter after my Mom passed away. He's been watching us since forever, that's how he knew everything about us." "But G, why did killed JD? He was our friend." G drops his head, "Zeke, honestly,

164

I have no answer for that. I guess I just did what I felt I needed to do to protect my family." Hugo's livid, he flips the desk over, grabs Alexis, putting his knife to her throat. "Gabriel, my son, you disappointed me. I spent many years watching over you, protecting you. I come to Lakeshore to be with you, just as I promised in my letter. I wanted to give you everything your mother couldn't, and you choose your friend over your own Father?"

G's breathing heavy, he stands in front of me. "You're not my fucking Dad, you just some Mexican cunt that got my Mom pregnant. If you wanted to be my Dad if you love me like you been claiming since I met you, then you would've been here since day one. But instead, you chose to abandon my Mom and me. Nigga! You ain't shit!" Hugo, using Alexis as his shield, slowly tries to ease his way back towards the stairs leading to the office. The sound of helicopters and sirens are in the distance but seems to be approaching quickly. With every step back

Hugo takes, G takes a step forward. Alexis is crying petrified of the possible outcome.

Hugo laughs, "What?! You little negro?! Am I supposed to be afraid of you? Your nothing without me!" Bear comes down the stairs with a shotgun in hand. Hugo sees him, "Right on time, my trusted dear friend. Bear, kill my son and then kill his friend. Show them what loyalty means!"

Bear cocks the shotgun, "FBI, drop the weapon.

Hugo looks stunned, his eyes widen. He shouts, "You're not FBI, you lie!"

Bear grins, "No, sorry Hugo. I'm Agent Fred Smith with the Federal Bureau of Investigations. I've been undercover for the last five years."

Hugo frowns, "No, no, NOOO!! I saw you kill that coward Ruiz!" "Ruiz flipped on Hugo, he was willing to give you up, but the information wasn't good enough to indict you. The whole Ruiz killing was staged in order for you to trust me! Loyalty is a motherfucker ain't it?" The sirens can be heard right outside the building, the tension is high. G's pointing his gun at Bear, Bear has the shotgun pointed at Hugo, Hugo stands between them both, with one arm wrapped around Alexis's neck, the other hand holds the knife to her throat. Managing to get to my feet and limp closer.

Tears begin to fall from G face, he takes a deep breath, exhaling slowly, "Bear, I can't let yo ole ugly ass kill my Pops."

Bear looks confused, "I'm giving you and Zeke a way out. Don't do anything that you'll regret G! Lower your firearm. NOW!"

G shakes his head, "Nah bruh, you drop yours!"

"G, this my last warning, DROP THE FUCKING GUN!" G fires a shot, Bear hits the ground squirming in pain. The shot seems to startle Hugo, he looks down at Bear rolling on the ground, moaning in pain. Alexis stumps on the tip of Hugo's toes, the immediate pain causes him to release his grip, and she runs over to help me stay on my feet. G looks over at us, sadness in his face, tears in his eyes. "Zeke, I love you brother. I told you I'm going to always have your back. Take your girl and get the fuck out of here."

"G come with us, please. We can get through this together."

"Nah Zeke, I've done too much to turn back now. I created this monster, now I have to end it." G wipes the tears away from his eyes. "Go do your thang College Boy." Limping over to him, I embrace him with a hug. I whisper thank you, he gently pushes me away, "Yeah, yeah I ain't with that gay shit my nigga." I smile, limping back to Alexis with my head down. G yells out to Alexis, "Aye girl, sorry about your fat ass brother, but the piece of shit had it coming. Make sure you take care of my homeboy. He loves you." She smiles through the tears, as we're walking towards the door.

Bang

Turning back to see where the gunshot came from, Hugo's body drops to the ground, G stands over him. Bang… Bang… Two more shots into Hugo. I turn and limp through the exit door.

Agent Sanchez runs towards us, "Ezekiel what the hell were you thinking?" I lift my head so he could see the physical and emotional pain before I continue walking past him. The Paramedic rushes over to me with a blanket, wrapping it around my shoulders, and leading me into the ambulance. Agent Thomas and Sanchez walks over to me and asks who still inside the building. Alexis crying says, "Hugo is dead, my brother is dead, and that FBI guy is probably dead too." They go grab a couple of their guys to go canvas the grounds, a loud explosion happens inside the building, flames are bursting out the windows. Agent Thomas runs over to the Firemen, he's pointing towards the building, I can only assume he told them that Bear is still inside. The Firemen scramble to get their equipment to fight the blaze. Waiting inside the ambulance watching to see who they bring out. I'm praying they walk out with G. A few minutes later, the Firemen along with Bear emerge from the building, Bear walking on his own will. He comes over to me, his arm bloody in a sling. "Zeke, I'm sorry I didn't step in sooner, I couldn't afford to blow this case."

All I care about right now is knowing if G made it out. "Did he?"

Bear shakes his head no. "I'm sorry Zeke, he didn't make it." I feel a part of my soul drift away from my body, I lay back on the stretcher, crying. Alexis holds onto my hand as they close the ambulance door and drives us away.

Ali Shakur

Three Years Later
(Announcer)

"There are ten seconds left on the clock. The Howard Bison's with the ball after the timeout, down by one. If your UNC, you have to know that Ezekiel will bring the ball up court. Do you trap him at half court or play man to man and try not to foul? Alright ladies and gentlemen, here we go! Ezekiel with the ball, six seconds on the clock, he loses his defender off the pick, he has an open look. The ball is up… IT'S IN! IT'S IN! The Howard University Bisons win!!! They win their first ever NCAA Basketball Championship with the game-winning shot by Ezekiel Miller! Wow! The scene is bananas! The fans began to rush the court! Let's get it down to Luke Grimes as he is courtside with Ezekiel Miller."

"I don't know if you can hear me over all the loud cheers Zeke, but you just made history. What was going on in your mind as that shot went up?"

"Coming out the timeout Coach told me to just relax and if it's meant to be it will be. Royce set a nice hard pick, I got a good look, it felt good when it left my hands. I'm just happy right now! Yeah baby! Yeah!"

I did it! I fucking did it! I won the National Championship. After everything I been through, I still persevered, and it's a feeling that I cannot explain. I move through the chaos of the crowd to get my fiancé and my Mom. Alexis runs up, hugs me while she's jumping up and down. Picking her up, spinning her around in pure happiness, and locking lips with her. My Mom's crying tears of joy as I move to hug her. "We did it Mom! We did it!"

"No Zeke, you did it baby! I'm so proud of you!" Jumping up and down with the rest of the team, giving high fives. I'm just taking it all in right now. Someone taps me on the shoulder, turning around, I'm instantly paralyzed! My heart racing with fear as I look into the eyes of something I thought I escaped. The terror, the fear. The face of death, a man with a crown tattooed under his eye smiles sadistically. The face is recognizable, it's one of the Kings from the hospital parking garage. Turning to get away, he grabs me by my jersey, causing me to slip and fall to the ground. He reaches into his pocket, my eyes widen. I should've known I wasn't going to get away. Getting back onto my feet, I plea for him not to do it here. He laughs, throwing an envelope at me before disappearing into the crowd. I quickly open it, it's a note! …

"You did yo thang College Boy! Loyalty always! Love you Pop Tart!"

"Our deepest fear is not that we are
inadequate. Our deepest fear is that we are
powerful beyond measure. It is our light,
not our darkness that most frightens us. We
ask ourselves, who am I to be brilliant,
gorgeous, talented, fabulous? Actually, who
are you not to be? You are a child of God.
You're playing small does not serve the
world. There is nothing enlightened about
shrinking so that other people won't feel
insecure around you. We are all meant to
shine, as children do. We were born to
manifest the glory of God that is within us.
It's not just in some of us; it's in
everyone. And as we let our own light shine,
we unconsciously give other people
permission to do the same. As we are
liberated from our own fear, our presence
automatically liberates others."

-Marianne Williamson

Ali Shakur

www.ingramcontent.com/pod-product-compliance
Lightning Source LLC
Chambersburg PA
CBHW052133170626
46812CB00004B/1387